Wind Blown Ashes

In Service to Evil, Volume 2

James R Steinhaus

Published by James R Steinhaus, 2024.

This is a work of fiction. Similarities to real people, places, or events are entirely coincidental.

WIND BLOWN ASHES

First edition. October 20, 2024.

Copyright © 2024 James R Steinhaus.

ISBN: 979-8227899484

Written by James R Steinhaus.

Table of Contents

Chapter I 1
Chapter II 17
Chapter III 34
Chapter IV 48
Chapter V 57
Chapter VI 68
Chapter VII 79
Chapter VIII 92
Chapter IX 101

Chapter I

Golden Needle's Caravan

Head held high, Ashes took a deep breath and marched out the same gate she'd entered through a few fortnights ago. But now, instead of naked and chained, she wore the robe she'd sewn last night, her hood up, a scarf wrapping her head, hiding her slave cut hair.

Thankfully, luck was on her side. Unlike home, many people in this town, both men and women, covered their heads, and some even faces, exposing only their eyes.

The other people making their way out of the city eyed her, then gave way once they saw the robe.

Her scarf hid her smile. The three black symbols she'd enchanted into her robe, moon, sun and triangle, rotated and moved about it from seam to seam. Not one person was interested in hindering a mage.

Stepping beyond that wall, more tension left.

No more whoring!

Glancing right, not far from the gate, she spotted a caravan that, from the look of it, was preparing to leave tomorrow.

Perfect. She headed for it.

Then froze in her track two steps later.

Two dwarfs and several gnomes sat at the common fire, mixed in with the humans.

That complicated things.

Few nonhumans lived in the city she just left, but not in the section of town she had worked. That section had been human only. She had almost no experience with nonhumans since laws forbid nonhumans from entering the kingdoms west of the mountain.

She sighed.

Those kingdoms were gone.

The only other human-only cities she knew of were the very ones Mistress Gru controlled. Going further east meant moving into cities with large nonhuman populations and her destination was an elven city. Taking a deep breath and bracing herself, she approached the half circle of wagons around a central cooking fire, her stomach tying itself in knots.

These, like the wagons in the caravan she arrived here in, were shop wagons, so this caravan would move slowly and stop and sell at most towns along the way.

Those nonhuman eyes on her as she approached sent a shiver down her spine.

She addressed the group as a whole. "I am looking for guard work as far as Kematree."

The dwarf, a little better dressed than the other dwarfs, spoke. "Mage? Headed for the Kematree Archives?"

"Yes, sir," she said to the black bearded, leather clad being.

"I am Rockhammer Silversmith, manager of the caravan's guards," he said.

The voice was as gruff as she had heard.

He went on. "The caravan manager is a Gnome named Ississine, but you can call him Golden Needle, which is what that translates into. He and his wagon are inside the city, won't be here until tomorrow. We could use a mage if the price is right but don't have a strong need of one."

Ashes wished she could read the dwarf better, but the meter of his speech was wrong and he didn't make eye contact the whole time he talked. Did all dwarfs do that, or was it just this one?

Rockhammer continued, "I can pay you half a silver crown a day."

She sneered. "Then you don't want much of a guard for that. For that, I only guard after we stop until wagons close up shop. I ride in a wagon. You give me a bedroll, and I have a place in a wagon to sleep."

A broken tooth, dirty bearded fat man, spoke. "Hell girl, you can share my bedroll," padding the bed roll he sat on.

"Kyayonday."

Ashes' hand burst into flame, and she turned to face the man, raising her hand to shoulder level.

Rockhammer spoke, "Crim, pack your bedroll. You're out of here. I can't have a guard in this caravan stupid enough to insult a mage to her face."

The man looked into Ashes' eyes.

She stared right back. Having come that far, she had to convince him she would kill him if he didn't leave, or none here would take her seriously.

He lowered his gaze. "Fine, I am going. There are other caravans."

Rockhammer turned to her, still not looking her in the face. "You can ride in a seat of a wagon, not inside, but you will need to sleep under a wagon, rather than in one. Four of them have mounts for a hammock under them. You get one of those and a hammock along with your bedroll."

Her first offer hadn't been what she had planned, but with modification would work and get her there safely. "Meals. And something better than porridge and soup."

"Fine, plus two full meals, but you will need to settle for a couple of pieces of fruit for your third one."

She nodded and held out her hand.

The dwarf just looked at her extended hand. "I'll get you a bed roll and hammock. Tonight, you can hang your hammock under the food wagon, and I will sleep elsewhere. Tomorrow, you sleep under Golden Needle's wagon. That is also the wagon seat you ride and where you spend most of your time on guard when we stop. He has mostly jewelry. Only a little of it silver and jade, the rest copper but enough silver that he is always a target. He is the one your deal guarding the caravan is with, and he will put it in writing, not shake on it."

He stood. Standing, he was still a head shorter than she. With an abrupt turn, he led her to the nearest wagon, which was the food wagon. Both the hammock and bedroll, which was a heavy double thick blanket treated on one side to resist water and dirt, that he pulled out for her, was new.

"The bottom of Golden Needle's wagon is like this one. Tie your hammock to these rings here." He pointed to two large brass rings hanging down. Opening a small cupboard, "This is my hammock and bedroll. There will be an empty one on Golden Needle's wagon for you to store yours in. Practice tying it now, because you will need to do it in the dark most of the time."

Without another word, he turned around and went back to where he'd been sitting.

She found out why she needed practice. If tied too loose, her bottom hit the ground. But too tight, made getting in and out of it difficult as she was right up against the wagon bed.

Once again, her butt was touching the ground when an older man with short gray whiskers set a plate with sweet potatoes, bread, and a quarter of a pheasant on it down next to her.

"Eat your dinner and when I come back for the plate, I will show you to trick to getting it done right, fast."

His voice surprised her, deeper than expected and with the same short, clipped cadence as the dwarfs. Was that the common way of speaking in the east?

That worried her. It would be far harder to blend in if her manner of speech was that different.

Distracted by the food the old man had sat down, she banged her head on the wagon bottom, getting out of the hammock.

The food smelled great. And surprisingly, the bread was still warm from the oven.

She bit into it.

It was delicious, better than she had had in weeks.

She tasted the sweet potatoes.

They were heavenly.

Even the pheasant had less of a gamey flavor than such birds usually had.

If all her meals were to be of this quality, she'd made a better deal than she'd thought.

The old man came by just as she finished the last of it and was sopping up the last traces with the last bit of bread.

"When word reaches him that you not only got him kicked out of the caravan, but now had his job guarding Golden Needle's wagon, Crim might try something. Stay near the wagons and don't let your guard down."

She swallowed. "If I know he is there, I can take him. My problem is if he surprises me."

"That sure of yourself?"

Putting far more confidence into her voice than she felt, she replied, "Certainly. Any reason I should not be?"

"Not that I know of, other than he is very good with his axe."

"Will the others in the caravan let me know if they see him or hear anything about him?"

The old man looked over to where the caravan guard master sat. "They'll tell me and Rockhammer. I'll pass it on to you. Name is Ho. Behind Golden Needle, I am senior wagon master here. I sell spices."

She raised an eye at that. Unless things were far different this far east, he would be the riches man in the caravan, though he dressed no better than any other person there.

"Thank you, Master Ho."

"Now let me show you how to tie that so you can quickly adjust it if it touches the ground. You start by tying a loop and passing that loop through the ring like this." He tied a loop.

**

A painful jabbed in her ribs startled Ashes out of a sound sleep.

"What are you still doing in the hammock?" said an angry, harsh, gravelly voice.

Fear mixed with anger flooded her.

"Kyayonday!" She said grabbing the stick poking her. Her hand turned to flame and half the stick to ash.

The little gnome jumped back, dropping the small staff he had been poking her with. Then in a sharper voice, "You're not Rockhammer."

"No," said Rockhammer, coming around the end of the wagon. "She is your mage guard. As you can see, she reacts to threats instantly."

"What's she doing in your hammock?"

Ashes let the flame die and started climbing out of the hammock.

"A hammock, good meals, and riding on your wagon, are all part of the pay I negotiated with her in order to keep your coin outlay down. She will be sleeping under your wagon, guarding you, from now until we get to Kematree."

"I see. I will be more careful waking her there then." He turned to her. "Mage, what do you go by?"

"Ashes."

His eyes shifted down to the charred staff he had been using. "I see. Well Ashes, all new sign-ons need to be at my wagon one candle mark after dawn. I will have the agreements ready to sign then. We leave right after."

Looking past the gnome, Ashes could see, by the pinkish tint to the eastern horizon, dawn was still a candle mark away.

"Rockhammer, come with me. We have a few things to go over before we start."

Standing, Ashes noticed her scarf had slipped during her sleep and quickly adjusted it. Had either man noticed her slave cut hair?

It was dark enough that the gnome had mistaken her for Rockhammer under there, so probably not. She cast a cantrip that sped up how fast her hair grew as she had last night. With luck, using that cantrip morning and night and her hair should be shoulder length in two weeks.

The cook was already serving breakfast to a crowd of people, though the sun wasn't up. Two different breakfasts, in fact. Most were getting bowls of porridge. She and a few others got the second pot. Last night, she had watched him set up that large pot with beans, herbs and spices, with some pork added, to cook over a low fire overnight. On top of her bowl of beans, she got bread baked last night.

They smelled superb this morning. If she had breakfasts like this one to look forward to, she was glad she had included better meals in her deal. The hot cider he handed her made that deal all the sweeter, and she took both over to sit near the communal fire.

After her demonstration last night and this morning with flaming hands, no one tried getting close to her. She considered how she had reacted with anger and magic both times. Both were signs she needed to more actively balance her scales. She had too much black in her grey.

Aside from giving her plenty of room, none of the others seem to give her actions a second thought. It was as if they expected her to roast people that irritated her.

Maybe they did. She thought about how she had viewed people that used magic before she started learning it herself. Being on a hair trigger might also be good for her reputation from what the dwarf had said. But she had to get rid of the anger.

Watching the sun come up reminded her of the last time she had watched it set all those moons ago, the night before the volcano. This was her best meal since then, too. Then, everything had changed for the worse.

Could this signal a change for the better?

Three men and one dwarf stood outside the gnome's wagon when she arrived a little early. Even the dwarf pulled away from her and toward the others when she joined the group. There was no hostility in it, but that action said she might be a guard, but she wasn't one of them.

The gnome, whom she assumed to be Golden Needle, opened the end door of his wagon and looked them over, interrupting that thought. The tiny, warty, gray-skinned creature, less than waist high on her, came out, pulled down a table attached to the end, sat a page on it and said, "Ashes, you are last. I have two contracts for you to choose from. Everyone else, put your mark on his one saying seven silver sovereigns per ten-day pay, payable at the end of the ten-day for guarding this caravan. Then report to the places Rockhammer assigned you."

The deep, gravelly, voice was strange coming out of that child-size person.

When they were gone, the Gnome rolled that one up and put two different ones down. "One is for the half silver a day all the way to Kematree with the terms Rockhammer negotiated, payable in Kematree. The second one is my offer for a silver a day all the way there, but with the added condition that you drive my wagon, also payable on arrival in Kematree."

She badly wanted that extra money, but aware of how much black she had accumulated was honest. "I have little experience driving a wagon and none on one with two mules. Nor do I know a thing about hitching them and care of them."

"I am moving the man I had driving over to another job, but he will still take care of hitching and feeding them. You are going to be in that seat anyway, so I want you to drive so my man can handle other things for me. For the first half a day today, he will ride with you, making sure you understand how to handle them."

"In that case, I'll take the silver sovereign a day to be a driver too."

He looked up at her. "Your tone says you are wondering why I am paying someone to drive my wagon instead of doing it myself. That shows you don't know much about gnomes."

She wondered why he thought that from her tone as it hadn't occurred to her, but answered, "No sir, I don't. Before today I have never spoken to one, and yesterday was the first time speaking to a dwarf. I am from beyond the western range."

"I see. I was saddened at your homeland's destruction. Another time, you might tell me more of it." He paused, then went on, "I have excellent vision over short distances, far better than humans. I can actually see the different thicknesses of the threads making up your robe just standing this close to you. But sitting on the wagon, I can't even see past the ears of the mules to the road. My wagon guard needs to understand my limitations outside the wagon. You are responsible for letting me know if you see something I need to know about."

She became confused. If his eyes were that good, how had he mistaken her for Rockhammer? That statement rang false, as did the false sympathy for the destruction of her home. Yet, she answered, "Yes, Sir." She wanted that money.

"Then sign, and get up there. We pull out as soon as my man Stone gets back from inspecting the rest of the wagons."

He raised an eyebrow when she picked up the contract to read it.

But he said nothing.

His script was so tiny she at first thought it to be a language she didn't read. **"Seaos."**

Once more, that cantrip helped her see what she needed to, not only lighting the page better but making the letters stand out.

She began to read.

At the end of it she said, "Good for the most part, but I want one change. You can hold most of my wages until we get to Kemetree. But I want one quarter of them each ten day when you pay the other guards."

"Acceptable." He took the contract and began making those changes.

She signed it Ashes of the West.

**

The sun had long passed its zenith when the caravan pulled into the commons of a smallish town little bigger than Cold Fork. Driving the third wagon back had distinct advantages, as the man no older that she, named Stone, told her earlier that morning.

It took little effort on her part to start or stop the wagon, as the mules just followed along, starting when the wagon in front did, and stopping when it did, unless she did something. She breathed in less dust.

The right-hand mule dropped a load approaching the commons, reminding her of an advantage of riding that Stone hadn't mentioned; not stepping in, and dodging, mule and oxen shit.

Stone hadn't stayed on the wagon seat with her long this morning. After all she had been through these past moons, she found it strange a youngish man not wanting anything from her, but he had been in a hurry to get away from her as soon as he knew she knew how to start and stop the wagon. Still, Ashes found it strange. The four other women in the caravan were married, as well as one of them being a gnome.

Nor was there a whore wagon for the unmarried men to visit. Gnomes didn't own slaves, and Golden Needle would not let slave owners join his caravan. But the moment Stone had been sure she knew what to do, he got away from her.

Much to her surprise, Stone climbed up the side of the moving wagon as she drove into the commons.

"Move over. I'll park it," he said with the same clipped accent Rockhammer used, and she became more certain that he didn't like her. She was unsure if his dislike was because she was a sorceress, or a Westerner. Either was possible. Her time as a whore had shown how many Easterners felt about Westerners.

Hanging the reins as he had taught her, she made room for him and he sat, taking them up.

She found out why he was the one to park it.

Getting mules to back a wagon up is far more complicated than just making sure they follow the wagon ahead. But he did it with ease, set the brake, then hit the side of the wagon with his hand. "All set, Ississine. You can come out."

Without another word, or even a glance at her, he jumped down and started helping Rockhammer direct the incoming wagons. There were a lot of those, as this caravan was twice the size of the last one she had been part of.

On hearing the bar on the back door being drawn, and it opening over the noise the incoming wagons made, she climbed down, using far more caution than Stone did.

"Ah, good," Golden Needle said as she came around behind the wagon. The gnome's deep voice rolled, croaked and hissed this time, making him hard to understand. He pointed to a chair he had set up next to the steps up into his wagon. "Change into something with more flash and more intimidating, then you sit there, and you escort in any customer who wants to enter my wagon. You make sure that only one person comes in at a time. We close up when the sun is still a hand above the horizon as no one buys jewelry that late. Then you follow me around as I visit the different wagon. This close to Lowford, I don't expect many, if any, buyers for my goods. None of the wagons with more expensive goods will do well the first two stops."

She let out a sigh. "I don't own anything with more flash. If you want me wearing such, then buy me the material and I will sew and enchant it, but I keep that as a bonus for wearing what you want. Keep in mind, serious players assume the more flash, the less power the mage has after a certain point. This robe tells them I am a sorceress, and little more on purpose."

"You need to look more impressive," he said in almost a cough.

"Then loan me some of your jewelry and take it back when you close up for the night."

He looked her up and down. "That will work, and I have just the things. Step inside."

Jewelry crowded every space inside that wagon, hanging all over and covering every surface. The clearest place being where his workbench was, and that looked to be pulled down to cover his small bed. But even that showed several pieces in construction. Had he been working while she drove?

"How much of this did you make?"

He hissed at her. "I don't sell things made by others. A gnome must be willing to vouch for the quality of anything he sells. How could I do so if someone else made it?"

Her eyes widened at that. The amount of jewelry she could see was staggering. To her surprise, he didn't choose from any she could see, but pulled open a box from under the workbench/bed. Instead of the copper and jade that covered everything in the wagon, this contained silver with assorted gems.

A large, exquisite silver and opal necklace went around her neck. He folded her robe sleeve close to her wrist, then used jeweled silver pins to clasp it in place. Then a dragon arm band went on her upper right arm. He finished it off with a silver head chain holding a small ruby over her forehead, on top of her headscarf, with three more jeweled silver pins to make sure it didn't come loose.

He spoke fast, hissing his words even more, making him hard to understand. Then he repeated it clearer and slower. "That should do it. Most people will believe that only a mage of sufficient power would be wearing these things on guard duty."

She saw herself in the half mirror he had mounted on his back door and gaped. Exotic, mystical and dangerous were the words that came to mind. Not one piece was over the top or out of place. She had to agree that she looked like a mage guard you would be cautious about, or even fearful of.

That gave her pause. If someone was going to attack this place, she was now the target they would take out first.

Her eyes narrowed as she realized that had been part of this gnome's point in dressing her this way. If she failed at intimidating people, she was to be their first target. That had not been her plan, and he was paying far too little for her to be the main target. Having read the contract she signed, she considered her option.

"No. it is too much. This exceeds the reasonable risk clause you put in my contract. If you want me taking this much risk and standing out that much instead of just being in the background guarding you, it will cost you more."

"How much more?"

She considered it. "Copper and jade copies of all the jewelry I'm wearing in addition to my current contract." Having a full set of jade and polished copper jewelry would help her present the right image at the library to get access.

His words were slow and deliberate. "That might actually work better as a guard. This may give the impression that taking my wagon would be worth someone's time, now that I consider it more."

He helped her remove the silver jewelry. He didn't raise an eye when her scarf came off with the last pin, exposing her slave cut hair. He just handed her three jade tipped copper pins to hold the scarf in place after she rewound it. Then, with care, he selected from that hanging about what she would get and put it on her.

She looked in the mirror. If anything, it was more tasteful than before, yet in its fashion appeared more menacing.

"Acceptable?"

"Yes."

He moved the things on his desk, pulled out another sheet of flattened Tia bark he used instead of parchment and wrote a different agreement listing everything she was wearing, on the spot, then held out his silver tip pen for her.

Once more, she read it before signing it.

Stepping out of the wagon, Ashes' shoulders relaxed, glad not to be so close to the gnome. She sensed it was mutual, and one reason she was to sit outside the wagon instead of just inside the open door.

Her instinct told her, and she had been taught as a child, that all non-humans were evil and dangerous.

Her mistress told her that was both right and wrong. It was wrong that all were evil. It was extremely rare to find truly evil elves, dwarfs, or gnomes.

But they were dangerous. They thought differently, had different things driving them and could take offense and the slightest cause, and soulless; they hit most human senses as demonic.

To the non-human, humans also came across as demonic; so demonic that many nonhumans used the same style of bargaining they would with a demon when bargaining with a human, expecting to be betrayed. Her mistress had even said that according to the lore of the elves of the deep-south islands, human were a class of lesser demons.

That view explained all the clauses Golden Needle included in her contract. On reflection, she realized that working for the non-humans was going to be more interesting than she first assumed. She took her seat and watched the others, a few of whom were already doing business with the locals. That was sparse and stayed sparse over the next few hours, with none approaching the wagon she guarded.

Golden Needle said something from deep in his wagon.

"If you were talking to me, I didn't understand. Can you say it again?"

"Fetch mine, and your dinner, from the cook. It is dinner time, so he should have it ready now," came out with fewer hisses.

Rockhammer approached her as the cook was piling food on two plates and started talking too fast for her to follow.

"Can you say that slower?"

"Tell Ississine that we can do his rounds just after he eats, and I will lock the place down. Any serious buyers have been here and gone already. Those left are only here because they have nothing better to do and have no plans to spend any silver."

Closing up before sunset with as few people as had shopped, didn't make much sense. Why had they even bothered to stop? They could have been three hours further along had they continued.

"Be ready," was all Golden Needle said when she handed him his plate, without her even telling him. She knew gnomes had better hearing than people, but that good?

Fear and dread appeared on the owner's face of the first wagon they approached.

Golden Needle held out his hand.

That fear turned to anger as the wagon master placed three copper bits in the extended hand. It was repeated at the next and the next.

Hired muscle, that is what she was, she realized. He may not be a money lender per se, but the job was the same. She was there to make sure the people that owed the gnome money paid up.

That shed light on why so many were unfriendly to her, especially the other guards. It also told her she would not make any friends here.

Damn. It dawned on her in a flash; it had been her confrontation with Crim that got her the job as muscle. He had this job. Rockhammer must have assumed she was challenging him for that job instead of just standing up for herself.

The last stop was the food wagon, who was just starting the bread baking for tomorrow's breakfast. Golden Needle handed the copper bits to the cook. At her raised eye, he said, "In the morning, before we start, you will collect the copper ingot from him. This will be jewelry before our next stop."

Once the gnome was inside and had his door bolted, she sat down in her chair and opened her spell book. She didn't have any warding spells memorized, but this was going to be the last night she slept outside without one. As time went on, the chances of one of the wagon masters wanting to get rid of Golden Needle's muscle would grow.

Eventually, her eyes grew tired, and she climbed into her hammock under his wagon. She wasn't sure, but this job might be pushing her more toward the black instead of helping her rebalance things. She knew breaking the contract would certainly do so. Once more, she had gotten herself into a lose-lose situation.

That didn't make for a restful thought before sleeping.

Chapter II

To the Library of Kematree

As Ashes struggled out of her hammock in the predawn light two towns later, she knew there was no way out of her contract without breaking her word. That had far too many consequences that she would not like unless the gnome did something evil. Gnome ethics, and human ethics, were not the same, according to her mistress's books. She was finding out how true that was.

She shivered with dread as Golden Needle's door opened as she packed up her hammock and bedroll. Without a word, she fell in behind him as he made his morning rounds.

His eye lit with delight at the third wagon down and the man sleeping under it. He poked the sleeper with the staff he had replaced the one she burned with. "Get up, you lazy human. Give me my copper bit and start getting ready to move out."

His gravelly speech was still hard to follow, but she was getting better at it. She hated helping him collect those one copper bit fines for people not being up, getting ready to move out by the time he left his wagon. The man glare with anger but paid the copper bit without a word. The latter she suspected was solely because Golden Needle had a mage backing him up.

Five wagons down, the spice wagon was closed up tight.

Golden Needle bang on its door with his staff, "Open up and give me my copper bit." He kept banging until Ho opened and handed him a bit, glaring at the two of them.

Ashes had no friends here. Not even Golden Needle. At best, he disliked her the least.

At the cook's wagon, he laid into the cook. "You had the fire too large. You don't need to build one up that everyone can put their pots in overnight unless they are paying for the fuel. Before you ever build one that big again, you pay me two bits for fuel first."

"Then it won't be big enough to melt your copper. Any fire I build big enough to do that is big enough to let other people cook in."

"Then I guess I need to find a more skilled cook,"

"Guess you do. Let me know when I can take my wagon elsewhere."

"You don't think I will?"

"I don't care if you do. I can have another place, at as good a pay, even here, though it might take a couple of days."

Ashes made note of him. So far, he was the only one to stand up to the gnome.

"You want your breakfast, or not?"

"Yes, you son of a rock lizard, give me my breakfast, and my copper."

He took his plate and copper and left.

"Here's your plate," the cook said once Golden Needle had left, his voice full of suspicion tinged with anger.

"Thank you. I am glad to see someone who stands up to him."

His voice stayed cold, but he replied, "Most of them dare not. Besides hiring enforcers, his clan runs nearly a third of the caravans on the most used routes, and a third more won't hire people that his clan has banned. I am an exception. My reputation is such that even others in his clan would hire me unless he could prove breach of contract. "

The way he said enforcers, she knew they would never be friends. Sighing to herself, she took her plate to the seat she sat guard in. Once more, she ate alone, and in silence.

Stone came by and without a word began hooking up the mules just as she was mopping up her plate.

That was her cue, and she climbed to the top of the wagon.

The moment those were hitched, he signaled for the lead wagon to move out.

A few moments later, the mule followed the second wagon out, without her needing to tell them to.

**

"Stop! thief!" grabbed her attention six nights later as she sat guard outside Golden Needle's wagon.

Ashes looked up from studying her book at the yell of the spice merchant.

The dim firelight made seeing the two boys running from him difficult.

"**Seaos.**"

Rockhammer made a grab for the two, but they dodged around him with practice ease, heading for the entrance and the wagon she guarded.

"**Hilcol.**"

She felt a sharp stabbing pain in her temple. The two had been further away and further apart than that spell was meant for. Forcing it hurt.

Both fell like birds dropped by a sling.

The door banged open next to her seat, smacking her in the head.

She went down.

"What's going on!" screamed Golden Needle. Then, seeing her on the ground, he shouted at her. "Get up, you useless droppings of a gecko."

Her head swam and looking at him, she saw double.

Rockhammer spoke from next to the two fallen boys. "The mage you just insulted, just took down the two snatch thieves that had dogged passed me. While she was recovering from the casting, you smacked her in the head with that door."

"Well, if she had been sitting in it correctly, the door would have hit the stopper on the seat as it was designed to do and not her," he added testily. Then looking at her again, "Can you get up?"

"Not yet. Using that spell that far away took a lot out of me."

Rockhammer examined the two boys. "Both have all their fingers. Thumb or pinky?"

Ashes spoke with anger. "Neither, or I walk. It was my spell that stopped them, so I get to say their punishment." She loathed cutting off fingers for petty theft, as the law required most places.

"Just what punishment do you suggest?" snapped Golden Needle.

She managed to prop herself up on her elbow. "Strip them. Give back the spices they stole back to Master Ho. Then divide everything they have between he and I. Leave them tied naked when we pull out for their family to claim."

"You think they have family here?"

Sitting up more, she looked back at the two. "As they are fairly well dressed, probably craftsmen's families."

"You heard her, Rockhammer, see to it." Golden Needle pulled his wagon door closed and slid home the bar with a thud.

Not one person helped her to her feet or back to her chair.

Her headache got worse sitting there, watching the guard strip and tie the young men.

Sometime later, Master Ho came by with a bundle and a steaming pot and two cups. "Not much. Gave you the better suit of clothes and all the carved charms they carried. I doubt any have any real power."

He poured the two cups. "Here's a steaming cup of tea for your head. Mages and healers commonly buy it from me. It's mostly black tea, with enough peppermint and chamomile added to remove the bitterness and let you sleep better. Cook heats me enough water every night. I'll start bringing you a cup by. You didn't have to put out that effort to stop them, especially when they were just on the edge of your range."

"What did they take?"

"Unicorn root. I doubt they wanted for what most cooks do."

Ashes could hardly believe she blushed at that with all the things she had been through. Raw, it was a mild hallucinogen and aphrodisiac; cooked, it neutralized many common poisons.

"So, you think they would have given it to some unsuspecting girl?"

He laughed, "No. Raw, is it bitter. Bitter enough that you need to really want that effect if you are going to eat enough for it to work. You don't hide that taste. Usually, a tiny taste convinces people, it's not worth it."

"I didn't know."

"I doubt they did, either. I suspect more than half of what I sell goes bad unused. Not all that many people cook with things that need to be neutralized, though enough do that I always carry some, especially for the gnomes."

She sipped the tea. It was rather good and didn't need sweetening.

He left, taking his pot with him and leaving her with a cup.

His cup, or the cooks, she pondered, looking at it.

She would find out tomorrow when she got her breakfast.

As she hung her hammock and climbed in, she considered that spell she'd used. With her medical book, and her understanding of that spell, she should be able to come up with a version that had a longer range and could effect people.

**

Golden Needle stood at the outside table attached to his wagon and checked off in his ledger every deduction of her pay for all moneys and services received. Her replacement stood there watching with a scowl on his face. That half-elf was cut from the same condescending cloth as Crim and would fit right in with Golden Needle's need for an enforcer.

Ashes raised her voice. "No, look it up again. We agreed that I got a bed and hammock as part of my pay. You are not going to charge me your inflated prices for them."

His new guard stepped forward.

Ashes pointed at him. "And if you don't call off your dog, I'm going to roast him, and you will need another."

"Bark, take a walk. Come back in a candle mark," Golden Needle growled out.

She grinned at calling a half-elf named Bark, Golden Needle's dog. She hadn't caught that name before.

"You sure, boss?"

The half-elf's sing-song voice irritated her even more than the Gnome's.

"Sounds like she is trying to extort more pay out of you than you owe."

Golden Needle snapped at him. "Don't butt into my negotiations again unless asked."

The whole demeanor of the half-elf changed to one of contrition. "Sorry boss. Taking that walk." He would fit in perfectly in her old job.

The gnome turned back to her. "My prices are not inflated, it is only a standard markup. There is nothing in this contract about giving you the hammock and bedroll."

She heard Rockhammer speak up from behind her. "That is because I gave them to her before you got here as a hiring bonus. It is even in my ledger saying that. The one you didn't bring out with you."

She hadn't known he was there. Rockhammer wasn't backing her because he liked her, it was because he disliked Golden Needle more. The whole caravan was like that, everyone disliking everyone else but the cook, and half of them didn't like him either.

"Fine, no deduction for the bedroll and hammock." He added a silver and three copper bits to her stack. "But these others, stand."

"That was the only one I hadn't agreed to, so yes, those others stand."

"Then sign your contract as paid in full and you can have your money."

She picked up his copper point, hand crafted jade pen, dipped it in the ink well and signed it.

"Two silver bits for this pen as a keepsake for fulfilling a contract with a gnome."

"Two bits! That pen is worth twenty."

"Not to me."

"If you want it, I'll go as low as ten."

"Most I can go is six. It isn't something I have to have."

"Fine, but only because you did such a good job."

She took that pen and gathered her coins into a small pouch, then picked up her pack containing her bedroll, books, and a few other things she managed to add. She hadn't had a good pen to use since leaving her mistress and she had a lot of writing ahead of her. Since she had known how much he had into it, he only made half a silver bit on her.

Only a few wagons down at Master Ho, she set her pack down again.

"I'm going to miss our evening teas," the elderly man said.

That, she knew, he was saying out of politeness. He didn't care for her, but felt he owed her. It gave her an in to getting what she wanted now. "Maybe we can share one more tonight when you close."

"You're not going into the city tonight?"

"I don't have a pass, and the fee to enter without one cost too much for such as I. I can't get one until tomorrow. Golden Needle ended the contract tonight instead of tomorrow knowing that. I was wondering if I could hang my hammock under your wagon tonight. I'll be gone before you get up."

"It has the mounts, but I have never used them. I have never hired a guard or driver, and I sleep inside."

"They should be fine. Maybe here is where you can find that apprentice you mention needing. He can drive for you and sleep under your wagon."

"Perhaps. You think you can get into the city before the sun is up?"

"No, but I can get down to the river, get myself and my clothes washed, and hang up my dress to dry. It should be dry by mid-morning, which is when I plan on trying to get that pass."

"Very well. I would love to have one last cup of tea with you tonight."

"About that. How much for a quarter stone's worth?"

**

Putting her comb and the rest away, Ashes longed for one of her Mistress's mirrors. Even with the spell she used each night to speed up growth, it was still too short for her taste, but at least wouldn't be mistaken for a slave cut and she could reduce her headscarf down to a tiny one. She tried without a scarf over her head, but could not get the jewelry that had been part of her pay to set right unless she set a small cloth there first.

Since she was stuck with a headcloth of some type, she had enchanted the small round red one she now used with a changing pattern based on blowing leaves.

Picking up her pack, she headed for the south gate of the largest, oldest city she had ever visited.

Lining both sides of the road stood tables with people hawking their services. No human got into this city without an invitation and a pass unless they paid a very high fee. Three-fourths of these tables were people offering work contracts, which came with a pass. She walked past those and found a letter service.

"Need a letter?" one old woman asked.

"Delivered to the Library of Human knowledge."

"I can get it to the door guards. But to get it to the admissions desk, you need to go three tables down."

Ashes handed the woman a copper bit, "Thanks for telling me who I needed to see."

A half elf sat at that table. Behind him knelt several goblins, each of the small greenish creatures wearing only a slave collar and pouch.

"Library letter?"

"Yes, please."

"My fee is three silver bits, two more for one of my runner to pay the gate keepers. My runners have been cleared so the library gate guard won't eat them as long as they have that fee. It will take weeks for a reply if you don't include the interview fee up front. That is 20 silver bits for a total of twenty-five silver bits."

The total, she was sure, was closer to fifteen. She was just as sure he wasn't going to haggle with her. It could take her days to find the right person to get it beyond the gatekeepers for a lower price. She handed him twenty-five silver bits, counting them out one by one.

"Name?"

"Ashes."

"Just Ashes?"

She raised her hand.

"Kyayonday!"

Her hand burst into flame.

"Yes, just Ashes."

She let the flame die.

He grinned at her and wrote notes on the sand tray on his table. "Who was your teacher?"

Ashes exaggerated slightly. "She refused to allow anyone to know her name." Partly true. She never once said her name, but it was written in the books she handed Ashes to study. "She sent me here to do research. The volcano of the west, happened below her home."

The half elf raised an eyebrow. "You were in the west when that happened?"

"No, but I saw it. I was in an inn in Overlook looking right at it when ash began to rise." Time for more embellishment: "Since then, the only name I have used is Ashes."

He made more notes in the sand tray. "I see, and the purpose of your visit. I have to have that in the letter to if you want to get past the front door."

"I asked my teacher about another fire spell. She said come here and research it myself like she had." Not exactly a lie, since this was the library her mistress mentioned using on many occasions.

He made another note in the sand tray. "I think I have enough now to write you a letter that will get you a fast response."

He opened a fancy ink well, and a goblin handed him a pen every bit as fancy as hers. With it, he wrote quickly and cleanly and in a language she could not read. Not just a few lines, but three full pages.

"What language is that?"

"Shyshakan, or as you would say, Green Sea dialect of the Elvish language. All the senior guards here use it, and all application letters as well as any official communication must be in a language they read."

He placed it in an unsealed scroll case and handed it and eighteen silver bits to a goblin. The guard ignored the creature as it trotted past them.

"You may as well get you something to eat. It could be half a candle mark, it might not be until evening. It all depends on who has the duty there and how busy they are."

It was advice Ashes followed.

**

As Ashes rested in the shade of the city wall, a goblin approached.

"Master Ammes has your reply and will give it to you now, or read it to you for an additional silver bit." The voice was deep, purring and masculine, the voice of a powerful warrior. It didn't go with that scrawny body and green wrinkled face.

She was finding non-human ethics troublesome, with all the hidden charges. Reading the response should have been included.

Did the human woman that sent her to the half-elf get a kickback?

Ashes closed the text she was studying, put it in her pack, and went to the table of the half-elf. To the untaught, people might confuse half-elves with elves, but once you have seen any elf of any type, you never make that mistake again. Twice elves had bought from Golden Needle. No human can mistake something without a soul, such as an elf, for something with one, as half-elves have.

Village elders taught that races that do not have souls were inherently evil and those with souls were inherently good.

Her mistress corrected that thinking.

While devils don't have souls, demons did. That was one of the several souled races that were evil. The belief that soulless were evil came mainly from how different they were.

She handed the half-elf the silver bit.

"Excellent news. The library sent you a pass and granted you an interview at once. For a silver bit, Kick will act at porter, and show you the way."

She sighed and handed him one of her few remaining silver bits.

Kick was a different goblin than the one who had fetched her, older and bent over.

"Is he up to carrying my pack?"

"As a general rule of thumb, the older the goblin, the stronger he is. His bones might pain him some. But he can defeat every other gobbling here with no problem."

**

Ashes found out what the half-elf meant about the gate guards not eating his runner. Hellhound guarded it. This library was exclusively for those that followed the Gray Path, and those Hellhounds would attack on sight any followers of the White Path. They hated the Dark Path almost as much, but could be trained to allow certain ones to pass unmolested, such as a goblin slave.

Ashes took a breath. If she had drifted too far into the black, one of those hellhounds would kill her when she passed within its chain's length. It appeared that two hellhounds covered every entrance. Kick looked back at her, grinned, then walked between the two beasts.

She followed.

Both growled at her as they had a Kick but didn't move.

The spell barrier they crossed walking under that arch, one designed to kill any dark mage powerful enough to pass the hellhounds, made goose bump crawl up her arms.

Kick walked through the next barrier that had the appearance of a pool of water.

Ashes swallowed and followed.

Her ring burned her hand. Once through, she looked down and part of the barrier covered her finger.

She heard a voice. "Should you trigger that ring here, you die and that within gets your soul. You must agree to this or leave."

Ashes took another deep breath. "I agree."

Magic settled over her of a type she could not unravel.

"Unwise," Kick said.

She wanted to know more, but Kick just walked on.

Only then did she realize the voice she had heard had been that of her mistress. She hurried to catch up before he passed the barrier of blackness blocking the next arch.

This barrier her mistress had mentioned to her. As the last one neutralized items of evil, this one neutralized holy items. A powerful devil lord put it in place.

Had a demigod put the one before it in place? Neither light nor dark wanted the other to gain access to this place, so the lords of each had been called on in the protection of it.

Kick set down her pack beside a door. "In here is your interview."

**

The gray-haired, dark-skinned fat woman behind the desk gave Ashes a disdainful look as she walked into the woman's office carrying her books under one arm. In a voice both icy and condescending, the woman spoke. "Most westerners are barely literate. You need to convince me you are not wasting our time allowing you access to knowledge you have no use or need of."

From her dress and manner, Ashes knew the woman was an Aristocrat. She also tasted of someone that never even completed their apprenticeship, having barely the power to pull off cantrips. But she did have the power to stop Ashes from going any further into the library. She placed the medical text she carried on the desk in front of the woman.

"That is the copy I made from my teacher's personal library. This is a second generation copy as my mistress copied hers from the original itself."

The woman opened it, then said, her voice even more frosty, "Impossible. The original was in a private library and lost over a thousand years ago when the place was burned. At best, she may have seen a first generation copy."

Keeping her own voice calm and on the quiet side, Ashes replied, "My mistress was quite old. I was her first student in centuries."

The woman sneered. "Who was this mistress?"

"I may not say. When someone that old and powerful doesn't want their name getting out, they can take steps. Steps that last past their own death."

The fat woman's eyes narrowed, and she looked at the book in hand. Turning the pages, she said, "Your penmanship needs work, but your drawings are passible. I will have one of the scholars run a comparison to our copy of this text, which is a first generation one. Nor have you taken care of this book. You would have very limited access because of that, if we gave you access at all."

Hardening her voice and speaking louder, realizing she had been using the wrong approach, she answered her. "That book doesn't leave my sight. It is rare and was stolen once already." She embellished, "That damage occurred in the thieves' possession. I am not letting my books out of my possession again."

The tone seemed to work, as the woman looked at her with more caution. Then the condescending attitude was back. "You will not be allowed to just look through whatever you want. Just what tome are you interested in?"

"Master Carroland's Observations on the Nature of Fire. I was working with a copy of it when my teacher sent me away so I would survive the volcano."

"That is a very advanced text. For someone of your age and background, I would recommend something far more basic."

The background of which the woman spoke, Ashes was sure, was her being a westerner. She focused on the candle, pictured it lit and started calling her magic exactly as if she was going to do the spell.

Soon there was a throbbing behind her eyes. That throbbing became a stabbing pain spreading to her neck and back as the magic built.

It became an agony, as if her whole body was on fire.

Without Ashes ever saying the word to cast a spell, the candle lit.

Exhausted, she slumped forward, barely able to keep from falling out of the seat.

The woman had stepped back from her desk and the candle. "Are you insane?" the woman shrieked at her. "Calling wild magic here! In my office!"

It took effort to speak, the throbbing behind her eyes still blurring her vision. "That wasn't wild magic. You should know that. It was using magic and my will alone, without a spell. Something my teacher insisted I learn. To call fire that way, you must have a very firm concept of what fire is, far beyond what some basic text might have. Only works such as I mention will further my knowledge to the degree I need."

"Don't you dare call magic like that again! You have no right to put others at risk."

Was this librarian that clueless? The only person at risk doing magic that way was the person doing it.

"I'll have someone show you to the cells. That text is the domain of Scholar Benz. He will see you tomorrow."

"It will be a few minutes before I can walk. Doing magic without a spell takes a lot of energy."

**

A day and a half passed before someone, a child, showed her from the cell that they had assigned her to Scholar Benz. Ashes tried not to stare. His long, wiry, white beard stood out against skin blacker than any Ashes had ever seen before.

His deeply wrinkled eyes narrowed as he looked back at her. "So you're the arrogant western mage that doesn't know any better than to call wild magic here."

She let out a sigh. "I didn't call wild magic. I used magic and my will, without using a spell."

"In its way, that is even more insane. More mages die attempting that, than calling wild magic. When wild magic goes wrong, you still have a fair chance to survive it. No one survives the backlash if their will falters."

"A fitting punishment for attempting it without the necessary will or understanding. I knew of no other means of quickly demonstrating that I understood fire well enough to need what she called advanced text. This is the third spell, and the most difficult one I have ever done that way. It is not something I plan to make a habit of."

The old man huffed, then opened a journal in front of him. "To cover rental of the cell, your food and access to the text you asked for, you will work here as a copyist from just after breakfast until the dinner bell. After dinner, you will be allowed two hours a day with the text you requested. You can start with the text on that desk. You won't get access to the one you want until tomorrow and only after I have gone over the work you have done today and pronounce it passable."

She didn't care for his tone, nor those limits, but had little choice but to accept.

At the desk she found a much-abused text with the title *The life and Magical Properties of the Black Mountain Toad.* Opening the text, she saw the words blurred from water damage. It didn't take long to see that the work use was archaic and hard to understand. If it was the original, then it was at least a thousand years old. She finished reading the entire page, then addressed Scholar Benz.

"This language is archaic. Am I to copy it accurately or in modern word. For an accurate copy, I would need to make notes under some words, as these were my best guess, and the original was too blurred to be sure."

"Normally it should be a true copy. In this case you can note under the title translation and reconstruction and sign it."

"Can I simply write, by the library staff instead, of signing it? Some of the translation I may need advice on."

"Mages." He said in a tone that showed experience with some people being reluctant to sign their name. "If that is your wish,"

"Then my first question. I have read the first page. It this about mountain toads that are black or toad for a mountain called Black Mountain. The way he wrote that first page, it could be either."

He looked at her, surprise written on his face. "I don't know, and I read ten pages to determent if we should salvage it or not. I had read it as mountain toads that were black, but it could well be toads from Black Mountain. Read the whole thing and see if you can determine that before starting."

"Puzzling through something that damage is going to take me at least two days. I will have nothing for you to judge and release the text to me tomorrow."

"Make notes. If I am satisfied you are making good progress, you can have access to the text tomorrow night after dinner."

By the time to quit, she was becoming convinced that it was toads found on Black Mountain and not mountain toads that were black but would need further study to prove that conclusively.

Dinner was with Scholar Benz in a small private dining nook near the kitchens. He was an excellent dinner companion and much of the dinner conversation revolved around that topic and how to resolve it, so there would be no confusion in her translation.

It was a great relief being treated as a junior colleague and not a whore or muscle.

Chapter III

Kematree and Beyond the Wall

After lunch the next day, a wonderful farmer's pie, delivered to her desk by the staff, Scholar Benz arrived back from his lunch and set three massive tomes on her desk. "I've spoken to Scholar Teach about your questions. These are three books from his section that he remembers that mention Black Mountain and may have answers."

Those questions hadn't been important to copying the text. She had just been trying to make dinner conversation using what she was working on. "I can read them if that is what you want, but that throws out getting this done quickly and you said my access to the tome I need, depends on me working fast."

"Right is more important than fast. Making sure the questions you raised last night are answered correctly is making sure you are doing it right. Wasting time isn't allowed. Taking the time to see that it is correct is to be encouraged. Just keep good notes on what you are reading. The simple fact that you asked those questions instead of just guessed shows you pay more attention than most that exchange copy work for access to research material."

Her interest peeked, she asked, "How else do people get access?"

"City residents may buy time to study a tome, but only if they are citizens in good standing. This library was supposed to be only for them. But that was when only elves lived here. All the way back in the beginning, this library needed a human staff since no elf, and few half-elves, can follow the Gray Path. They negotiated that the human staff may use it too so they could have a Gray library in Kematree to go along with the White one that used to be here at that time. So you see, signing it library staff is actually accurate. According to the law, you are temporary staff. You have six months to apply for and get a permanent place here or must leave the library and the city."

Not risking her life or freedom sounded great. "Can I get a permanent job here?"

"Not until you find a way to rid yourself of that demon attached to your soul."

That phrasing startled Ashes.

"From what the guardians have told our staff, the hold is still loose enough to be dislodged, but you don't have the power to do that yet."

"But I can stay here six months. Can I have access to the tome on getting rid of the demon latched on to my soul after I finish copying the tomb on fire?"

"That text is not in my section. After you have copied the tome that you've made arrangements with me to copy, you may apply to the master of that section. I will introduce you to her. If you do a good job for me, I will even give you a recommendation, but she lets few outsiders into her section. You would have to convince her."

"I see."

"You do have one advantage. She is so strict because so many turn to the dark path after getting access to her section. You have on a ring that will pull you to the Dark Path if you don't learn control of it or how to remove it. In your case, having access to that book lessens the likelihood, not increases it. She will see that as you needing the access to stay on the Gray Path."

Goose bumps formed on her arm. "So, I need that book to stay on the Gray Path?"

"What, no. There are many many ways to dislodge that demon. But all require you to become more powerful. The book just contains information to make it easier for you. The demon is weak, and its hold slight, according to the guardians."

Ashes breathed a sigh of relief, and Scholar Benz crossed the room to his own desk and opened the tomb he had been working on before leaving for lunch.

With a sigh, she opened the first of the massive text he set on her desk. By dinner she had come to the conclusion that the Black Mountain in this text and in the one she was copying were two different mountains in two different lands. This text was no help to her answering those questions at all.

**

Placing the last of her notes in the small hearth fire and watching them burn, this newest spell echoed louder in Ashes' mind than any spell she had ever memorized. That was a sure indicator it was stronger than any spell she had. It was also the first, purely combat spell. Even her energy darts spell was more for knocking fruit out of the high branches than an effective weapon against an armored knight. Her teacher might be able to batter a man to a bloody pulp with her own energy darts spell, but all Ashes would accomplish with hers would be to put a couple of bruises on one and pissed them off royally.

She could feel those three balls of fire her spell would release, straining to be set free, each able to roast a man in a heartbeat. Though she hadn't tested it, and wouldn't until she left the library and the city, she was certain it would work.

It had better. A spell containing this much magic would kill her if it didn't.

"I take it that you have finished your research and will no longer require that tome," Scholar Benz said, looking up from the tome he was working on.

"Yes. Since I am not going to be allowed into the section I need next, I will be leaving soon."

"About that. She still will not allow you in. Only mature mages, set in their ways and power, as she put it, may enter her section. It isn't personal. She doesn't grant access to the young and immature." He paused and took a deep breath. "But she has given me a single text she feels would be adequate." She watched him grimace before going on. "The text is very disturbing. You must keep your notes with the text, and she will read those notes each day. Using your notes, she will oversee that the spells you are creating are for your protection, not an effort to increase your power."

He stood and went to his satchel on the table and opened it. From that, he took out a rather large leather book-carton.

He opened it.

The evil and power of the tome smashed into her. Her finger throbbed.

"This book has forty-eight pages written on a single side. The reason for only one side being used as it was written on the backs of living elves using demon's blood who were then skinned alive to make this book. It is one of the weaker books in her section."

Ashes swallowed.

He unbound the string holding the book closed.

Her finger throbbed more.

"You are to use this table, not your copy desk. You are to study no more than one page a day, not touching the book itself. I will be the one to open it to the correct page for you each day and close it." He went back to his desk, sat down, and began to work on his tome again.

Forcing her breathing and pulse back to normal, she approached the table, then turned back to her desk for her writing supplies and the stool. She made sure everything was set up there correctly, even to the point of checking that the wicks were all trimmed on the lamps before seating herself before that text. The script was tightly written and not all that neat.

Bile rose in her throat at the thought that the writing had been larger, but the skin shrank after being taken from the Elf's back.

She read the first page's heading.

Tips on Torturing and Imp or Lesser Demon for Information.

**

Ashes woke in terror, her blankets sweat soaked.

At least this time she hadn't awoken screaming, as she had the first night after reading a page of that demonic tome.

Heart still racing, black night filling the room, she climbed out of bed and fumbled to the door.

Dim light in from the lone oil lamp burning in the hall entered her room. That feeble light helped her get her near panic back under control.

Stumbling into the hall, she grabbed the rushlight from the table the lamp sat on.

Hand shaking, she lit it, giving thanks that the staff added those to this table after her first night's screaming woke people.

There was no point trying to go back to sleep, even if dawn was a long way off. She'd learned that the first time. Letting out a deep breath, she grabbed one of the assistant's robes they provided her, three more rushlights, and headed for the well room.

Her rushlight flickered as once more, an invisible watcher entered the hall, sending yet another chill down her spine. These air elementals would call the guardians should they see anything suspicious. She didn't think they liked her and went out of their way, making the air colder whenever she was about before dawn. At least two were in the well room with her dropping the temperature maybe more before she was done cleaning up and putting on a new robe.

They abandoned following her as she descended to the next floor, and the dining hall.

Heat returned.

She made her way down the hall to the dining room.

"More bad dreams?" said the young woman, the baker's apprentice, already kneading dough for the morning bread on the big tables there.

"Yes."

"Tea's on the stove and there is still yesterday's bread back there. Help yourself."

She gave the girl a smile. "Thanks."

Ashes walked through the door to the kitchen, grateful that only the apprentice baker, a girl of maybe fifteen, was in this early. She was also thankful that the girl was willing to part with some of yesterday's bread. That leftover bread was, after all, part of an apprentice's take-home pay.

Bread and tea in hand, she returned to the dining room.

"If what you are studying gives you nightmares, why do you persist?" the young woman asked as Ashes sat down near her.

She sat in silence, considering how much to tell the young woman.

"Or is that none of my business?"

"It is none of your business, but I'll tell you part of it. I have a curse. What I am reading are some of the things that are in store for me if I don't get it removed. That is all I am willing to say about it."

That was the truth as far as it went, but far from the reality of it. The book was evil and cursed to drive anyone who is not evil, insane, if they manage to read more than a few pages. By Scholar Benz handling it, but not reading it, and her reading it, but not handling it, they avoided that. But there was still a cost.

"Then I hope this helps you remove it." With that, the young girl let the subject drop. It wasn't a moment too soon as the baker came in, scowling at the two of them.

That was Ashes' cue to head for Scholar Benz's section, though he wouldn't be in until well after dawn. She still had access to two of the books he had had her copy. Between those two and what she already knew, she had a fair chance of coming up with an insect summoning spell before she left, using all this premorning time to research it.

**

Ashes burned her notes, again. This time, relief filled her as two different scholars watch her do it. She dearly wished she dare remove, and burn, the three spells she came up with from these notes, but didn't dare while she wore that ring.

Chances were, those spells wouldn't even help.

Having read that book and made those spells, she feared that ring now more than ever. Her mistress should have taken it from her even if it required taking her arm. A child such as she had been, could not make a rational decision on such a thing, and that decision should have been made for her. Ashes had no clearer sign that her mistress didn't like her than the fact she hadn't taken that ring.

"It isn't nearly as hopeless as it seems. Nor is Durgon's Option called for," Benz said, appearing to have followed her thoughts.

She shivered. "No, I am not yet ready to have my soul sacrificed to one of the Gods of Light to keep me out of the abyss."

Scholar Astin spoke. "Maybe you should before it is too late. Having your soul trapped in an altar is far better than being the possession of a demon, even an imp. If you call on that imp, that will no longer be a possibility." She paused to look at Ashes. "You will call on it. Something will force your hand. Seven times that imp has gotten the soul of the person who called on it as those diamonds testify. Less than one Gray sorcerer in a thousand becomes powerful enough to remove such a ring. Sorceresses of the Gray reaching that level are even rarer. Most have to dedicate themselves to either Light or Dark to get that power. You have no chance now at Light, and Dark would mean something worse than an imp gets your soul."

With that, she picked up the tome and left.

Scholar Benz sighed, then spoke. "Scholar Astin, having charge over such powerful tomes, has made her skeptical of other's abilities. She hears almost only of failure, and little of success. Though I have been accused of being overly optimistic since I am surrounded by tomes of those that succeeded. You yourself have already succeeded well beyond what you expected in entering the library. Instead of a single spell added to your spell book, you have added six."

"I wish I could stay longer and research more. And I wish I had arranged to copy that text instead of just studying it. There is material for dozens of more fire spells in it."

"Once you have been settled some place for a few years and have your own library, contact me and together we'll petition the council for a longer stay working here. It would be far easier if you write a tome worthy of being copied and included in the library, yourself."

The thought that she could write something that they would include surprised a laugh out of her. "I can see it now, *Ashes notes on mending clothes by hand*."

He laughed. "Not with that title. However, *Mending clothing as practice by those destroyed by the Great Eruption,* would work as a title and be of interest to many. As not only a survivor of the Great Eruption but also a survivor of towns no longer there, there are many things you could write about that could get your tome included here and get you access to more tomes."

The thought of scholars a hundred years from now reading a tome she wrote instead of just copies sent a thrill down her spine.

"Once I have a permanent place, I'll get started on that."

"Make sure you do a good job on it. And it would be best if you have removed that ring before you apply to return."

**

One last look in the small mirror satisfied Ashes that her newest look worked well. The half mask hid her eyes perfectly while a large scarf wrapped her head, hiding even her race. Every bit of her was covered, hiding her fair skin. She was as ready as she would ever be. She hefted her pack and walked out of her cell.

A young human boy, maybe eleven years old, well dressed, approached her as she entered the dining hall. "Sorceress Ashes?"

"Yes."

He held up a scrap of parchment, and trying to sound important, said, "I am to be your escort to the city gates since you have no pass."

She smiled down at the child. "Then lead the way, good sir."

The trip through Kematree was longer than Ashes remembered, and her pack heavier than it had been.

On getting close to the gates, her young escort said, "I'm not allowed outside the gate. I am to watch you pass them, then report back to Ma; I mean the library."

"That's fine." She smiled down at him again, ruffled his hair and handed him a copper bit. "You watch me leave and run tell your ma."

Shifting her pack to a more comfortable position, she joined the crowd heading out.

With several still ahead of her, a whistle sounded, and a guard's lance came down blocking the way through the gate.

"Move to the side, people, you know the drill," barked the man leading the gate guard.

Not knowing the drill, Ashes followed the rest of the crowd in clearing away from the gate. She caught bits of her neighbor's conversation and looked down the road away from the gate. Two finely dressed elves with a guard of half-elves came down the road. According to Scholar Benz, the population of elves was exactly what it had been five thousand years ago, but the city was ten times bigger, and each elf ten times richer.

Ashes got a good look at them, as they pass not more than seven paces from her. Taking into account what Scholar Benz said, for all their finery and guards, these two would be near the bottom of the social level for elves of this city. The two walked with a closeness that said they were a couple, but for the life of her, Ashes could not tell which was male and which female.

Goosebumps covered her arms by the time they passed, and she understood all too well the wars so many other races had with the elves. Despite knowing very well that all elves but Dark Elves served the Light, every fiber of her said evil, kill it.

Glancing around, she saw she wasn't the only one that felt that way.

The guards clearing everyone back so they could pass suddenly made more sense. It hadn't been because all elves were rich, privileged, nobles as she had first thought, though that was true. With this much fear, it was for the safety of the elves.

All those rules and restrictions on outsiders made more sense, as did how protective the half elves were of their elven kin, who were the lifeblood of this city.

Her eyes found her young guide; face filled with fear.

Why would a mother who could afford to dress their child that well send them out alone to risk facing that level of fear?

The guard held them until after the couple was through the gate and they and the escort awaiting them outside of those walls mounted and rode away.

Nor did the people rush to get out once the guards allowed it.

Stepping under the arch leading out, Ashes knew she would know far more about this city and elves before she ever came back here again.

**

Turning right exiting the gate, Ashes meandered through the tables and a handful of interspersed small tent-stalls lining the road. In time, she came to the midpoint between this and the next gate, where the caravans were required to park. Tables, and the few tents, lined the whole way from the gate and continued on past this campground around the city.

"Any of these heading into the desert to O'freindwel?" she asked the half elf standing guard at its entrance in his worn and tattered tabard.

He sneered and his voice dripped with contempt as he replied. "No. One left for Old Friends Well, the first of the human cities to the south two days agone. I expect none to start forming for a ten-night, or more."

Ashes read manuscripts written by humans four thousand years old calling it O'friendwel or a version of that. Only some of the elves, and the half-elves, still called it Old Friends Well. It was his tone, and using Old Friends Well, that convinced her that her choice of destination was right. They would look down on her in any place that had the longer-lived races like elves, gnomes or dwarfs. The human run desert city of O'friendwel or the Land of the Eighteen Kings beyond the desert was her best bet.

Looking at the three caravans there, Ashes knew he was correct, and she had been a fool for asking. All three contained a lot of nonhumans of one type or another, so wouldn't be heading to O'friendwel.

So much for Plan A, she sigh, and continued down the road to put Plan B into action, glad to have taken time to develop Plans A, B, C and D while still in the library.

Not one of the tents she had already passed was suitable, so she pushed on, hoping it was Plan B and not Plan C.

Nearing the next gate into the city, she approached a herb woman offering cures in front of a tent. The condition of her tent, and clothes which covered her to the same level Ashes own covered her, suggested that she knew what she was about.

"What can I do for you, deary?"

Human, as Ashes suspected; and the voice and phrasing pushed Ashes' estimation of her age to past childbearing age.

So far, so good.

"I need several things. I am a mage healer who needs to expand my knowledge of herb healing and need a mentor in this. I need someone to share their tent while I wait for a caravan to O'friendwel to form. One with someone that isn't interested in demanding carnal pleasures.

And I need a place that I can work my healing. For all three, I offer a third of all coins I get while staying there."

The woman's voice became harsher. "More often than not, mage healers mess up as much as they fix. I am forever mixing up things for fixing what they messed up."

Hearing that tone, Ashes turned on all the charm and flattery she could. "I agree. Most mages learn a spell or two, then apply them badly over and over, whether they are the right ones to use or not. Magic should be saved for things herbs are not appropriate for, not as a replacement for them. I was in the library improving my magic so I may heal better. Now I need to further my knowledge of herbs. My mentor died before she could complete that part of it."

The older woman cocked her head to the side and pulled open the tent flap. "Let us step inside and discuss your proposition further."

It only took Ashes eye's a moment to adjust when the tent flap fell as plenty of light filtered in through the thin fabric.

Removing the scarf covering her face, then pushing back her head-covering, revealed slate gray hair and confirming Ashes guess about her age.

Some of the tension flowed out of Ashes seeing a kindly face and she responded by removing one of the pins holding her own scarf in place and letting it drop, showing her face. She couldn't push back the head-covering as the woman had unless she took out all the pins holding it in place.

"You are quite young for a mage, and pretty too. I can see why you are cautious in looking for older women to share a tent with. Most men will demand more in their tent if they get a good look at you."

"It made getting here difficult. Nor can I return. The volcano saw to that. I must further my herb and healing studied here, and move on, instead of returning home."

"Excellent delivery. You have the sound, and the look once your scarf is gone, of a westerner. It might even be true."

The tone was kind, but cautious and skeptical.

Ashes adjusted her approach to reveal a bit more of her travels. Taking on a quiet and somber tone, she said, "My mentor foresaw the volcano and sent me to the town of Overlook on some made-up pretense. She was too old for that journey herself." Ashes knew better than to tell all, even to someone with as kindly a face as this woman, but knew she had to reveal some of it. "I am from the west, and I am a healer mage, and I watched my home destroyed. As you have guessed, my traveling companions demanded favors of me to accompany them."

"And she told only you of the coming volcano she foresaw?"

"She didn't tell me she foresaw it. That was in a letter waiting for me there. She didn't like people. Had I not done certain things for her and passed certain test she would have let me die with the rest. She was not a nice person, but felt she owed me the chance to live, but gave me not a coin more than I needed to reach Overlook."

Ashes gaged the older woman's attitude and went on, "Nor had she given me sufficient spells. I had to get to the library here to get more. The trip was brutal, and men did thing to me I have no wish to talk about, but I made it, and I have more spells."

Now came the tricky part. "I need more herb lore, though. Many of the herbs here are different than found at home. To keep your tent and clothes in good repair and not be starving, you have to know what you are doing. Please teach me."

The woman laughed. "A good story, and likely mostly true. But all you really want is a safe place to earn a coin and a place to sleep while you wait for a caravan. Sitting in a tent versus sitting by the side of the road will get you more customers. That is easy to see. Here's my counteroffer. I decide who sees you while you sit outside my tent. You only do things, herbs won't cure. I get several of those a day I have to send on to healers. You help me move my tent and stock every day as the law requires I do. You can lay your bed roll here but provide your own food. I get two of every three coins, not one of every three. If and when we have time, we can compare what we both know about herbs."

Ashes made her a counteroffer. "You will have most of the customers. To provide my own food and to replenish any supplies I have to use, I need at least half of what coins I earn."

"You're trying my patients, girl. I am already late moving my tent. You help me move it, and if you don't break or spill anything, we have a deal, and you can keep half the coins you earn."

Chapter IV

Finding Passage

Pulling three large sacks from under her bedroll, the old woman handed two to Ashes. "All those herbs fit in those two sacks. But have a care not to crush them, making them fit. If it appears you will crush things, then pull everything out and try rearranging them. You just do the herbs. I'll pack the rest. All but the tent fit in this bag, but only if put in, in the right manner. Start with the eight boxes outside. The lids are under them."

The old woman fixed her scarfs over her head before she pinned back the curtain over the door.

Ashes covered her own face.

The boxes, more or less long, deep trays, were easy to load four to a sack, and still left each half empty. Using care, she added each of the bags of herbs outside to the sack, stacking them to take up as little room as possible in them. Once that was finished he went inside for the more expensive herbs.

The old woman had the sack she was doing already half full.

Ashes started loading those herbs in the sack outside. There was still a lot of room left when she finished.

"Good job. That is the level it should be considering what I sold yesterday," the woman startle Ashes as she was closing up the bag.

Ashes looked up as the woman pulled a three-tone whistle from her pouch. She blew it, fluting it from the different tones in some pattern.

"A wagon should be here to move us and restock my stores shortly after I finish packing. Since I buy from him most every day, it is to his advantage to move my tent and sacks for free, but you will need to help load and unload it into his wagon."

Soon the sack the woman was working on was full and it joined the two Ashes had filled. With a practiced hand, the woman removed the poles of the tent one at a time, folding it in on itself, and it too was soon folded up next to the three bags.

When the woman bought a meat-pie from a vender pushing his cart past, with reluctance, Ashes dug into her few remaining copper bits and did the same.

A shiver went down her spine as she handed it over. How long would it be before she could pay for such a trifle and not remember that at one time that was all men paid to have her?

Just as she was licking the last of the juices from the pie from her fingers, an elderly half-elf in bright clothing pulled up in his mule-drawn wagon and started speaking elvish, and the woman answered.

Ashes hated not understanding what the two spoke of. The conversation continued as he jumped down, and began handing the old woman herb bag that she added to the two large sacks, each of which she handed over silver coins for before he handed her another.

A healer herbalist would be ashes best bet for when she set up in the next town and seeing those coins exchange hand only confirmed that. She had mainly wanted a good place to sleep just as the woman had said, but she would pay good attention to what the woman had to say about the different herbs.

Cinching the sack closed, the woman said, "Help me load these up. He has someone hold a prime location for us halfway around the city, but if we want it, we need to hurry."

All three sacks were heavy, too heavy for either of them alone to lift. Who did the woman usually get to help her? Was having Ashes help her saving her coin?

**

"Start putting up my tent. I'll arrange my outside display and grab us a few customers," the woman told ashes as the wagon pulled to a stop.

Ashes sighed, climbed down and started pulling the tent and its poles off the wagon.

Neither the old woman nor the driver offered a hand to help her move that heavy load.

Sitting down one of the bags, the old woman said, "There are people that target you when setting up. They figure I will give them a better deal so I can get back to getting set up. Sometimes they are even right, but I always make it appear that way. It lets me sell them far more than they had planned on buying. Especially gnomes. Those deformed toad-lizards are constantly trying to screw other honest merchants over, and always buy more than they planned if it appears they are screwing you over on the deal. But we won't see them on this side of town."

Despite not liking her time working for a Gnome, Ashes knew that they were even less inclined to steal from you than humans, but kept silent.

The tent was simple and straightforward to set up, designed for one person to set up if too heavy for one person to easily get it into place.

"Good job," the old woman said, caring in the bag with all the inside stuff as Ashes put the last back pole up. Not one person had shown to buy the entire time she had been doing it. "You can set your own pack in here too, but don't roll out your bedroll until we close up. We will likely close up early. This side of town has a weak evening sales, but makes up for it by having more people shopping outside the walls in the morning."

Just then, their first customer showed up and the old woman stepped out, closing the flap on Ashes.

Ashes listened from the other side. Fortunately, it was a common eastern human language and not an elvish dialect.

She instantly knew that this wasn't a candidate for her healing spells. As she listened, her doubts of the woman's herbal knowledge grew, but her respect for the old woman's ability to sell grew. The man left with eleven small sacks of herbs for his indigestion, only two of which Ashes thought were likely to help at all.

It was almost the same selection of herbs for aging joints that the next person wanted the woman recommended then and sold them. By the time the sun was setting, Ashes recognized the pattern. She changed one or two depending on what that person's needs were, but was selling the same general mixture, half of which did no real good or harm. Everyone got something good for cleaning out their insides. Ashes recognized that three-herb combination as one her mother always used for that. That was three of the eleven. Two more were for sound sleep and two more for sore muscles and aching joints. Taking them when you didn't need them did no harm, but how much good they did when not needed was questionable.

Switching from elvish which her current customer used to something Ashes could understand, the woman said, "Ashes, can you come out here? I have your first customer here."

A very old half-elf woman sat in the back of a broken-down donkey cart, leg propped up a massive boil on her foot.

"Scorpion wasp sting?" Ashes said, seeing it.

"Toxic lasher."

"Almost at bad. The spell just to pull out the stinger is one silver sovereign. You can keep using a poultice and drain the poison over time that way or pay a second silver sovereign for a second spell to draw that out. You will need to pay my partner here a third silver sovereign for a mixture of herb to wrap it in if you want to heal in a way that doesn't cause you pain for years to come."

Her voice rang bitter. "The temple told me to come back tomorrow. I stopped here for something for the pain. If you can fix it tonight, I will pay your high fee."

Ashes bowed to the woman, then said. "Temples are always first come, first served. Each person can only do a few spells in a day. If you are not there early, they say come back tomorrow. It is always thus. Especially with difficult spells such as these."

"Truth," the woman said, relaxing some, pulling out three silver coins.

Ashes relaxed, relieved. Even agreeing with someone who bad mouths a local temple could bring them to your door. Especially if you were doing healing in competition to them. Another unwritten rule is never undercut the temple's price. She might get away with that healing bar-slaves, and customers, but in the market her prices had better be inline or greater than theirs, hence asking a full sovereign for it.

As the wagon pulled away, the herb woman said, "I think this may work out. You go buy us dinner, and I will start closing up."

**

Days later, the setting sun lit the old half-elf as the three of them drank tea outside the old woman's tent. "So it is agreed, you will escort my brother-in-law and his wagon to O'friendwel for nine silver sovereigns, one third of it to be paid in herbs after he makes his purchases?" said the man that kept the old woman supplied.

"Once again, no. That is only the price if you are providing acceptable food and a tent for me to sleep in while on route. If I must provide my own food and shelter, it is six more silver bits. You haven't agreed to provide those things."

"You are asking too much."

"If it is too much, your wagon isn't carrying anything valuable enough to be worth hiring a mage to guard it."

"How much of a guard is a healer going to be?"

Making sure there was nothing that would be damaged, Ashes raised both hands and spoke. **"Kyayonday Doma Seeyton."**

A cone of flame formed from her hand and three roaring balls of fire burst forth from the mouth of the cone and arced across the cleared field.

"I may prefer healing, but I am equally well equipped to do harm," she said, hiding the fact that, that was the first time she had actually done the spell she had spent so much time researching.

The old herb woman looked like she had swallowed a frog despite her face covering. Ashes had been inching to do that every time that old hag spoke to her as a common servant, despite all the magical healing she had been doing.

The old half elf looked out in the field, then back to her. "Your price might be acceptable, but with a further condition. You hide a small cask of Muri in your bedroll, so it is either with you or in the wagon, and deliver it to the Priest of Tears temple there. It must always be in your possession, and no one is to know you carry it, not even my brother-in-law."

The old herb woman's eyes bulged at the mention of Muri, but the half-elf herb supplier dealing in it didn't surprise Ashes one bit. But was it really a priest he was sending it to?

"Muri raises the price to twenty silver sovereigns, and I will only do it on a single condition. Such I will only carry from one priest to another. You have to get me a pass into the city, and we go to the Kematree temple of the Priest of Tears and he gives me a writ saying I am transporting it for him, and the temple puts a holy seal on it that will destroy it should any but one of their priest try to open it. It is vial stuff, but that temple makes legitimate use of it."

"Wise beyond your years. That can be arranged. The night before you leave, there will be a man with a pass for you at the eastern gate. He will conduct you to the temple and back."

"The temple gates only. I will not enter that building."

A visible shiver passed through the half elf. "Neither would I, or the guard that will have your pass. But the temple is used to that. They have a forecourt inside the gates to the outer wall that is not inside the temple itself. You will meet the priest there."

"Then when you pay me half up front, we have a deal."

He didn't try to argue paying half up front and counted out ten silver sovereigns on the spot.

Taking the coins, she said, "Make it very clear to your brother-in-law I get a good tent to sleep in and good food. I ride not walk. And the only service being rendered it guarding him and the wagon from highwaymen."

"It will be as you say," he said, standing up and showing more respect to her than any other time.

Once he boarded his wagon, the old herb woman said. "Food of the Gods and the Priest of Tears. I had thought better of you than that."

"If there is anyone that I would trust to handle Muri, it is the Priest of Tears. Despite their reputation, they are on the side of light. They only use it in very specific rituals."

**

"So, you're the brother-in-law of Karomain the herb merchant," she said to the sixteen-year-old human boy with just a few whiskers on his face sitting in the described wagon at the campsite.

He grinned, then jumped down, "Only in how elves count such things. My grandfather's sister is married to his great uncle. Both were tossed out of their families for it and are long dead. The fiction that we are related helps with taxes for his family and fees for mine. He doesn't have to pay the servants' tax if I work for him if I am a relative and the pass for me to visit relatives is far cheaper than the pass to deliver cargo."

He patted a white silk roll on the wagon behind his seat. "Got you a brand-new silk tent. I was told that if you damage it, the difference in what I can sell if for in O'friendwel comes out of your pay. Don't get too worried, it is a sturdy tent, and it will take a lot to damage it. You demanding a good tent made pops, add ten of them to the cargo I'm selling in O'friendwel, so both of us will have new tents this trip.

They really love elven silk tents there, so it is a good, profitable addition. Have you set up an elven tent before?"

"No," Ashes said, eying the energetic young man.

"Then let me show you how. They are both harder and easier to set up than regular tents. They are harder because they have to be laid out perfectly. No short cuts. They are easier because if you do that, you just pull on the center cord until the tent unfolds completely. If you pull on the cord and it isn't laid out right, it gets tangled in a way that can take hours, or even days, to undo."

Ashes smiled behind her face-cover. The boy was a flirt. "Go ahead and show me. So you are doing this trip alone?"

"Third time doing it myself. Second time Karomain has hired a guard to ride with me. But I have been doing this route with family since I can walk. Two more trips and I will have enough to attract a wife to do the trips with me."

"A worthy goal. Is there a girl you are after?"

He blushed, and his eyes shifted to a different wagon. "Yes, there is. But her father has other plans. I need to prove to him I can make a profit time after time. My fee for taking this wagon there is room to put the six end boxes on the wagon, plus food. By the way. Your making a point of it has Karomain buying the higher quality meals from the food wagon for both of us this time. I should be able to keep him doing that all the time now. Thanks."

Ashes fell in love with the elven dome tent and understood at once why it had to be laid out perfectly. Pulling the center line created tension on the multiple cords, pulling hollow tubes together raising the tent. But it if not laid out right, that tension not only raised them in the wrong order but being out of order kinked up the cord inside them. She had a cantrip that could straighten that out, but most would not be able to and would need to spend hours working their way to it.

"You caught on to that fast."

"I am a sorceress. That means I have to do many things in a precise fashion for them to work." She looked at the sun. "I will leave my pack inside the tent. I have an appointment in the city soon and my guard and pass should be at the gate."

"I'll keep an eye on it."

She waved her hand muttering the cantrip under her breath and a glowing rune appeared on the tent flap. "Do keep people out of it. They will regret entering if they do."

His eyes widen, "I will, Mistress."

Ashes was glad the face-cover hid her grin. The flash rune did nothing more that tell her someone had entered, and even for that, she had to be inside the tent. But it looked impressive as hell.

**

The trip to O'friendwel had to be the most relaxing travel she had ever had. Helping a sixteen-year-old boy impress a father had been fun too, and made her wish she had had such suitors. But to have such, you needed a father and mother that cared about you the way that girl's parents cared about her, and not one that saw you as a burden that they are stuck with.

No one in the entire caravan had suspected she carried Muri or Food of the Gods, as the common man called it. And she had not needed a major spell the whole trip, combat or healing.

Chapter V

O'friendwel

Relaxed in a way she hadn't been since leaving her Mistress, Ashes looked on the town of O'friendwel in wonder. There are many larger human cities, and many more important, but there may be none that are older, and few buildings here were more than a single story tall. There are hundreds of different conflicting stories about who and why it was founded, and Ashes doubted any of them were true, but even the oldest maps the elves or dwarfs possessed showed a human town in the desert here. No other place in this desert had wells that never dried.

"Make sure you remove all those glyphs before we get to town," said the young man driving the wagon.

Ashes giggled. "I will. Wouldn't want you peeing your trews." Then after a pause she said, "Again," and giggled some more. Then she went on, "But I don't need to. That type of glyph only last less than a day."

He grinned. "You scared the hell out of me. And nearly everyone in the caravan."

She smiled back behind her face cover. The screaming demon glyph was part of why her trip had been so uneventful. It is a harmless cantrip but if you break the glyph, an illusion of a demon came out of it screaming. It was a bad illusion, and it only took people a moment before they knew it was fake, but it can give you a bad fright.

Most of the caravan had thought it a great joke on him when he opened her tent flap to get her up and the screaming demon jumped out at him. But No one risked messing with her tent or his wagon since then and made sure to accord her the respect due a sorceress hired to protect a wagon.

She looked back at the town they were entering. It didn't match what she had imaged from her reading. For one, the majority of O'friendwel was outside its two walls and the caravan camped right in among those building bordered by four stables, and not in the desert as she thought they would. An aquifer brought water to a fountain for those stables and her caravan to use for free.

"You can have two more days of using the tent here if you need it."

"I might. After delivering that cask I was entrusted with, I need to make nice with the leading healers here to keep from stepping on the wrong toes."

"I can get you a start on getting in with the herb women here. Their main supplier be contacting me later. Most of this is for him."

"Thanks." Helping him get in good with a potential father-in-law was paying off.

All the temples were inside the second wall as the outer one was called, including the Priest of Tears temple.

She found that the second wall was only a wall in name in many places but for one factor. Whoever had warded it when it was built, had done a superior job as traces still existed pushing evil away. Even someone gray like herself felt an urge to be outside them. It made meeting with the healers more complicated, but it meant she could only set up outside that wall in the poorer parts of town.

She was thinking about that when she came to the Priest of Tears temple sooner than she expected from the direction she had.

Damn, it didn't have a forecourt.

She could not enter. Just entering was consenting to a purge, and that was something she could not survive with her ring on. Even knocking on the temple doors was out. She had no choice but to stand there waiting until someone entered or left that could take her message to the high priest.

**

The blazing sun crept across the sky, and her throat grew parched. The city wards kept pushing on her and even more so her ring as she stood there waiting for someone inside the temple to notice her. She was getting irritated.

After the sun had crossed a third of the sky, an older woman came out and Ashes addressed her.

"Can you take a message to the High Priest? I have a package for him from the High Priest of the Kematree temple."

The woman shuddered. "I have just undergone a purge. I have no wish to undergo another so soon."

"If you just underwent a purge, you have little to be purged, so it will be less. Even so, I will give you one silver bit to take him the message that I have a package for him."

"Let's see your coin."

Ashes held it up, considering how much more she would offer if the woman said no.

The woman squinted at it. "Kematree mint. Not as good as some, but still good enough, but not to the High Priest, I will tell an attendant."

"Very well," Ashes said, handing over the coin.

The woman raised her voice. "You heard the woman. She has a delivery for the High Priest."

"Then she can take it to his office," a voice came back.

Ashes had had enough. That attendant had known she was out here waiting and not done a thing. She yelled at the door. "I am going back to the caravan. If the High Priest isn't there by nightfall, I will assume that the package has been refused and return it to the High Priest of the Priest of Tears of Kematree temple. I'm done with your games."

She turned around and stormed back to the camp.

**

When the sun dropped behind the tallest buildings, Ashes wondered if she was going to have to make good on her threat. Then a commotion approached the camp.

The High Priest and a dozen lesser Priest entered the camp.

"How dare you demand that I attend you," a magically enhanced voice boomed.

Furious Ashes held up the package in her left hand.

"Kyayonday."

Her right hand burst into flame. "One more arrogant outburst and I destroy your package. I have been cursed. If I enter your temple, I die. Even going past the outer walls of the city is uncomfortable. Your people left me standing in the hot sun outside your gates, then tried to make me come inside. Give me one good reason not to destroy this package."

"I will kill you if you do," the man roared.

Ashes moved her hands closer together.

His voice became panicked. "No, don't."

"Your oath now, that you will not seek vengeance on me, or I destroy it and we see how your power matches my magic, and which of us dies."

"What. How dare you?"

Ashes moved her hands even closer, so that the flames licked the edge of the cask.

Now in an even greater panic, the High priest said, "I swear, by all the gods of justice and the right of Purge, no vengeance."

Ashes let the flame die and extended the package.

The high priest approached slowly and took it. "You are truly cursed so you cannot enter?"

She held up her right hand again and nodded to the ring.

The priest's eyes narrowed as he focused on it. After a time, he said in a soft, even kindly voice, "You haven't used it. We can still free your soul of it, but you are right, doing that would kill you. It is a step you should take before it becomes too late, and nothing can free your soul. An early death is better than a longer life and the torments of the abyss."

"My teacher not only wore it but used it, and yet was able to free her soul of it. In time, I will free myself of it."

"If true, your teacher was a very formidable person. I wish you luck on it. But don't use it until you have that kind of power yourself."

Ashes watched him and the rest of his priest leave. Would he cause her trouble if she stayed?

**

The last person Ashes expected to see as she got ready to close up her poor-quarters shop was the High Priest of the Priest of Tears temple, pushing his way in. It had been a quarter of a year since their run-in.

"What may I do for you, My lord?"

"It is not my fault; I kept my word."

Confused, she said, "My lord?"

"You need to run for it, now!"

"What are you talking about?"

"The Grand Sorceress of Light, Calashandra Ohsaland, is coming here in the morning. She means to kill you! You have to run now!"

Ashes squeaked, "Me? A council mage? Why?"

"Your ring. She summoned me to her home and asked me if you truly had a demon ring. I told her you had never used it. But it didn't matter. She means to see that ring destroyed and the demon in it locked away for all time. Even if she has to kill you to do so. Your only hope is to be so far away by morning she can't come after you. She has responsibilities here, so if it will take her more than a day to catch up, she can't come after you. That means you have to be at least half a day away by morning. It is against her code of conduct to hire someone to come after you, so if you get away now and don't come back, you will be safe."

For a moment, she thought he might be lying. But no, despite their run-in, he was here to warn her of her danger. Looking into his face, she was sure of that.

"Damit, everything I have is in the shop and I owe people for some of this. Even if I run, those will send people to collect on that debt."

He sighed. "That I can fix. Give me a list of your creditors and amounts and I will have one of my priests see that all of this gets divided up to cover your debts, and none sends anyone after you."

She had to run. She had no chance of surviving an encounter with a three-hundred-year-old White Council member, even a very junior one. After handing him her ledger, she began stuffing her three books, a few items of clothing, her bedroll, and her small herb bag into her carry pack. It was all she could carry and move quickly.

"How can I cross the desert?"

The priest handed over a water skin and small sack. "This is usually reserved for priest I send out. If you take only one swallow from the skin, it will last you sixteen days. The water is blessed in such a way that one swallow is all the water you require in a day. Put a wafer in your mouth from the other bag before taking that swallow and your hunger will be gone for the day, too. Unless you waste too much time, that is more than enough to get you across the desert and into the forest belonging to the human kingdoms."

"Thank you."

His eyes took on a distant look. "It may have been one of my priests that told Calashandra of your ring. I know they both attended a dinner earlier that day. This is all I can do to make up for that. His family connections makes him untouchable. You are lucky. Tonight, both moons are full and already in the sky, but you need to hurry. You must be gone before she realizes you are fleeing. I must get back and make sure someone doesn't go and tell her you have been warned." With that statement, he turned and left.

Ashes tied both the waterskin and pouch of wafer to her belt and hefted her pack.

It wasn't fair.

She had a real chance at a good life here. She had a herb and healing shop, good contact for supplies and had even started to make a couple friends.

First, she had to flee a black sorceress and now one of white, neither of whom she had done any harm.

Why did this keep happening to her?

Life just wasn't fair.

She closed her shop door for the last time as the shadows of the building stretched out long before her.

**

With the smaller of the two moons already up and the sun setting, sand crunched below Ashes' feet. At least this time she had proper footwear, something she had lost when the men of the dark sorceress had raped her nearly a year ago and only this month replaced.

She sighed. Once more with no choice, she fled a town with few combat spells memorized. Over the past weeks, she had transitioned to mostly healing spells. Even most of those were gone, as she used them all earlier in the day.

She turned and faced the ancient desert town one last time before darkness and distance swallowed it up.

Damn that intolerant White Council and their endless crusade on evil. Why did they even bother having someone station all the way out here?

Next time, if a powerful mage called the town home, she would move on quickly, and do nothing to draw attention to herself. She didn't really need a large town anyway, something the size of Cold Fork would do just fine. Towns like that would love having a healer-herbalist in their town.

A jackal's howl rang from the north.

A closer, more menacing howl returned it.

Her blood went cold as their hunting yipping started.

She froze, her breathing hard and fast. One fireball spell and one fire lighting spell, and she would be out of spells.

An ass braying started, and the yipping took on excited tones.

Her heart pounded. The jackals had cornered their prey, and it wasn't her!

She broke into a run, away from the sound, hoping it was a wild desert ass and not some traveler on a burro, but her pack threw her off balance and she nearly fell.

Should she discard it?

The ass screamed and was cut off.

She swallowed, fighting down her fear.

No, she should not discard her pack. Her chances tonight might be better without it, but she would not make it across the desert should she discard it. Furthermore, without her books, her options became cleaning woman or tavern wench again.

The sounds the jackals made tearing into the ass carcass and fighting among themself got fainter and fainter with each step she took, and her fear, less and less.

By the time the second moon rose, and the night calls of the insect and lizard started, she could no longer hear them. These night sounds comforted her. Like the woods back home, if the night sounds stopped, danger lurked.

When half the night had passed, and she heard a desert cat fighting a pack of coyotes, she relaxed furthered. If such small predators fought, it was a good indication that the bigger, more dangerous ones were absent.

The larger moon was still a third of the way up the sky when the east started to lighten and the sounds changed to early morning sounds. Ashes sighed. From its position and phase, she would be out of the desert before the long, dark, moonless nights arrived.

When the sun came up, the nighttime chill quickly disappeared. No longer chilled, the beauty of the desert and the long shadow she was casting across the sparkling sand it took her breath away.

As she walked, the shadow length decreased and soon sweat beaded her brow under her scarf.

She stopped and began doing what she had only seen done once on the way to O'friendwel.

Laying her bedroll out and covering it with sand in a way she could get under it was far harder than she had thought, and the process of covering it to the right depth took much longer. Sweaty, covered in dirt, she ached to drink that magical swallow but need save that until she woke and not drink it until right before she started off.

With a sigh, she sat down and opened her spell book with the sun beating down on her, making her thirst worse. She dare not sleep without memorizing at least two combat useful spells.

When she closed her book, she felt better for it. If she was far enough away that the bitch didn't come after her, she had a fair chance of making it across the desert alive. She lifted the sand covered blanket and wormed her way in.

Sleep came in moments.

**

Her blanket being pulled startled Ashes awake.

Terror flooding her senses, she put her hands out and shouted, **"Kyayonday!"** Flame enveloped two jackals, setting her blanket afire. It wasn't enough to seriously hurt them, but they aborted their attack and fled to the bushes.

The pack started yipping. She could see that there were a lot of them that had been quietly sneaking up on her.

Despite her desperation, she focused on the closest large knot of them and spoke. "**Kyayonday Doma Seeyton.**"

A cone of flame formed in front of her hands and three balls of fire emerged from it, flying straight for three different jackals packed close to each other, engulfing each in a far hotter flame than her first panicked spell.

Their blood curdling death shriek cut the night.

Jackals fled, yips now filled with terror.

Night?

By the gods, she had slept too long!

Her hand went to her head as she spotted her headscarf torn to pieces a few steps away.

When had that come off?

"**Seaos,**" she said and started searching the ground near it.

One scrap still had one of her jade hairpins. Of the rest of her jewelry on that scarf, she saw no trace.

By the lords of hell, how had her scarf been outside her bedroll?

First things first, now that she had a moment, her parched throat and empty stomach demanded attention. Keeping a watchful eye out, she pulled the pack out from under the blanket still half covered in sand and got the wafer and water skin the priest had given her out of it. As instructed, she chewed a single blessed wafer, then washed it down with only a swallow of the blessed water. Both left an unpleasant tang in her mouth, but her thirst and hunger vanished.

The jackals howled, startling her. They hadn't gone far.

After shaking the sand out of her bedroll as best as she could, she put it in the pack, then put it on her back and looked once more for any of her head jewelry.

The next howl was closer.

Why in all the names of the lords of light and dark did those damned jackals need to be between her and the caravan trails? Having used up two combat spells, she didn't dare use the others to try to force her way past. Even if it worked, it would leave her helpless should she have to face a different foe.

With an exasperated sigh, she abandoned her search for more of her jewelry and turned south and started deeper into the desert, away from the well-traveled route.

The howls changed to yipping, and the pack kept pace with her.

The larger moon came out.

Though they kept some distance between them and stuck to the shadows as much as possible, those nasty beast paced her.

But when that moon reached its highest point, the unmistakable howl of a sand ghoul cut the night, turning Ashes' blood cold.

In a rush, jackals forgotten in her terror, she dumped her pack in front of her.

Careless of what it was, she tossed everything aside.

Finally, she got to her small sack of herbs. Tearing that open, she dumped them into a new pile. Panic faded as she found the small bit of Mary's Wort she had.

"**Kyayonday!**" she snarled, pointing at a small dead shrub.

When it burst into flame, she tossed the Mary's Wort into the fire.

The howl came again.

Her magic can't stop a sand ghoul. She hoped that the text her teacher had her read was correct or she was dead.

Chapter VI

Out of the Desert

Somewhere out in the darkness, the sand ghoul's howl became a shriek of pain.

Ashes' heart thundered in her ears.

The ghoul shrieked again. It was further away.

The breath she had been holding exploded out of her mouth.

That had been close.

Too close.

All ghouls required far more magic than she had to stop them, but sand ghouls are among the worst. That sandy skin reflects all fire, lightning or cold based attacks, usually right back at the caster more often than not.

A shriek came from even further away.

She wished she understood why burning Mary's Wort would drive ghouls away shrieking, but it did. There were plenty of old wives' tales of why it worked, but, according to her teacher, no evidence that any were true. Supposedly, it would flee for three days. Then, likely as not, it would go after the person that drove it away if it could, according to what most text said about using Mary's Wort. She didn't plan to be near enough to it to find out.

Another deep sigh escaped her lip. Jackals, and now a sand ghoul diverting her further and further from the beaten path.

Grabbing the stuff she had just dumped into the sand; she started putting it back into her sack

When she finished, she looked up and saw the pink of predawn in the eastern sky.

She took a deep breath and let it out slowly.

Most of the night wasted, and what travel she did get done, was south and not in the direction she needed to go, east. The burnt smell of the bush plus the bit of Mary's Wort she had added to the fire made this place safer than most to camp.

So be it.

After laying out her bedroll, she pulled out her spell book and went to work re-engraving the spells she had used into her mind.

**

Pushing back her sand covered bedroll, Ashes squinted into the light glaring off the sand from the setting sun, the desert heat still enough to smack her in the face but nowhere near it daytime high. She finished extracting herself from the heavy sand covered roll and stood.

Shifting her eyes to the ground, she found no track she hadn't made last night.

Perfect.

Nothing big had prowled about as she slept.

Facing the direction she needed to go, she readjusted her travel plans. The scrub trees appeared to be closer together and greener off to the southeast. Not exactly opposite the direction that the sand ghoul had run, but still close enough.

A shiver ran down her back. She had no intention of being anywhere near that ghoul when the Mary's Wort wore off.

Opening the pouch the priest had given her, she took out her second wafer. She grimaced. It tasted worse than the last one.

So did the sip of blessed water.

Was that on purpose so you didn't try to depend on the god's blessings?

It was a real possibility. Some gods were like that.

She fought down another sigh. It was time to pack and to cover as much ground tonight as possible.

**

By the time the sun sank below the horizon, the shifting sand had turned into hard packed sandy ground, and she began searching for a game trail.

"Seaos."

Once she invoked that light gathering spell, finding a game trail didn't take her long.

Though predators hunted game trails, traveling them was usually safer and faster than going without any trail. Those trails existed because the ground they went over was easier to travel than the surrounding ground. Now she could make far better time.

**

The sun, rising only a finger's width above the horizon, lit a beautiful thicket of green trees just ahead of her.

By the gods, she'd reached a seep. It was the wrong season for such seeps to have water, but from the health of these trees, she suspected this one was usually wet all winter.

Relief flooded every muscle. Burying herself here to escape the sun was not needed with so many large green trees doing such a fine job of shading the ground. Once she laid out her bedroll, made a small smoky fire to discourage animals from coming too close, she pulled out her medical text and began reading it once more, pondering the possibility of creating yet another spell she had been contemplating as she walked.

**

The next night, Ashes once again traveled without incident, making excellent time along the well-traveled game trail.

To her delight, the sun cresting the horizon revealed that the trees were now close enough that she could continue walking in the daylight.

With her stomach threatening revolt at that taste, she ate the wafer the priest had given her and marched on.

She kept walking.

Well past midday, the game trail crossed a cart track.

Ashes stopped. She had made it. She had crossed the desert alone and lived.

But which direction to follow those tracks?

**

As Ashes entered the tiny village the wagon track led to with the sun only a few candle marks above the horizon. Every person around stopped what they were doing, suspicion written in every look and movement.

Not that she blamed them.

Mages were dangerous and unpredictable. Her dirty and trail-battered condition, combined with her mage robes, would strike fear into most villagers.

There was no getting around that.

With caution, she approached a weather-beaten old woman leaning against a fence post that appeared angry instead of fearful and bowed deeply to her. "I beg your pardon, Matron, I need to know where I might buy food, water, and cloth-n-needle to sew a new robe. I just spent four days fleeing a sand ghoul, and I fear my robe is a lost cause."

Rage filled those old eyes, and she shrieked, "Sand Ghoul, you brought a sand ghoul to our village?"

"No, Great Elder of this village, I did not," Ashes cautioned. Then said in a deeply solemn manner, "Four nights ago, I burned Mary's Wort when I heard that howl in the night getting closer. It fled one direction and I the other. It is many days to the northwest now. That is another thing I would ask: that was my entire supply of Mary's Wort. I have coin."

The woman relaxed some, but the anger was still there. "I have Mary's Wort, enough I can sell you part of it. At this time of year, no one would have spare cloth that they would sell you for a robe. The best I can do for you is sell you my extra embroidery needle and thread. I can sell you beets for your dinner, and there is a stream just two marks further down the trail. You have a pot?"

Ashes took note; the old woman was not offering to sell her a cooked meal or let her use the village well. There was little help for it. Fixing her robe would have to do. Few would help her until she look less disreputable. But there was still a possibility. "I am afraid I did not pack one. I did not expect to travel the desert alone, fleeing a ghoul, when the priest sent me out into the desert on a quest. I expected to join up with one of the caravans. But beets will be fine. I'll just roast them over a fire. Anything is better than the blessed travel wafers the priest gave me before sending me out."

As expected, the reference that a priest had sent her, softened the old woman's expression.

"A priest should know better than to send someone alone into the desert," the woman spat.

"I don't think there was any choice about that. The quest specified a time that I had to leave, and no one was leaving at that time," Ashes said, leaving out that the quest was to get away from the crazy white mage. "When the powers declare you leave at a certain time, you leave then or suffer."

Ashes watched the anger go down more. The brown old woman pointed to a milking stool. "Sit. I'll get you your Mary's Wort, beets, needle and thread. This time of year, there should also be some cattail near where you will get your water and clean up. Make it two silver bits and I will toss in a few flakes of soap."

What Ashes was asking the old crone for was worth less than a dozen copper bits. She knew that the old woman wasn't going to bargain. Nor could she just look elsewhere, as she could have in a larger town. No villager would undercut another for an outsider.

She removed two silver bits, handed them over, then took the indicated seat. After tucking them into her pouch, the old woman headed into one of the nearby huts.

Looking at the sun, she realized she had been walking for a full day now without rest.

The old woman wasn't gone long, but at least she came out with a generous helping of both the beets and soap flakes. "Just go on right out the other end of the village and just before sunset you will reach sweet water creek. A cart takes two days to make Fisher down that path. You can likely do it faster."

The message was clear. Take the food and go away.

**

Sun in her eyes as it touched the horizon cast deep shadows when Ashes came upon the so-called stream. It was nothing but a gully, created by seasonal rains that still had some water flowing through it; A wash that hadn't gone dry yet.

And their bridge, just logs, packed with mud, set over it.

Yet, after the desert, it would do.

Sighing with relief, she set her pack on the hard packed ground, climbed down the waist high wash, scooped up water in the palm of her hand and quenched her parched throat.

Wonderful.

Only a trickle of water flowed, but only a few paces from her, someone had dammed it with bricks so that the water rose to knee level beyond it for a place to do laundry.

Her luck held. Near that dam, driftwood littered its bank.

Perfect.

It her next to no time to have a sizable pile next to her pack, and a smaller one further away.

With the last of the sun now gone, she pointed. "**Kyayonday.**"

Flames shot from her hand, engulfing the wood in the smaller stack. She counted to twelve, then let the magic die.

The wood kept burning.

Bone weariness hit her.

She wanted to sleep; but needed to get some things done first.

With a sigh, she dug out what the hag had given her from her pack. Half her beets she set in the outer edge of the fire. The others would be lunch tomorrow and she returned them.

Then she looked around carefully, eyeing the shadows suspiciously. "**Seaos.**"

Nothing there.

Still, she would only strip down to her under-shift.

The robe ripped more as she pulled it over her head.

Holding it out, she examined by firelight.

It was a mess, barely more than tattered rags held together by threads. How had it gotten that tattered?

Best to wait for dawn to do what mending she could, she told herself. Soap flakes in hand, she headed for the tiny pool to clean what was left of her robe and herself.

**

After days on those god wafers, that hot beet sent waves of pleasure through her as she bit into it. She devoured each and every one with relish.

Placing her hand on her head she determined that her hair should be dry enough to go to sleep without becoming a mess soon and the robe draped over the bush near the fire should be dry by morning.

Great.

Ashes put a few more sticks on the fire and pulled out her spell book. She had two spells she needed to replace.

Book in hand, she dove for the wash before she consciously realized what was happening.

Fire engulfed her camp as five balls of fire exploded there.

She popped up shouting. "**Kyayonday Doma Seeyton.**"

Three of her own balls of fire arced back at the mage that had attacked her.

He dogged, but not enough. Two hit. They enveloped his shield but could not reach him.

His laughter filled the air. "I thought you more dangerous than that."

Her pulse racing, she turned and ran.

His voice intoned, "**Kyayonday Doma Seeyton.**"

Her terror spiked. She jumped from the wash, landing on her side, and kept rolling, clutching her spell book to her chest. Ashes realized it had been hearing those words in the distance that had her diving that first time.

The wash exploded in fire. Everything about his spell felt the same as hers, but with more power. Another fact her mistress had been right about, mages kept coming up with the same spells over and over.

"Escaped again, did you?" came from further away than that laugh had been.

In answer to that, she jumped to her feet and headed out into the scrub at a run, grateful her feat still had most of their calluses.

"Not so fast, **Hilcol Salma.**"

Ashes staggered, fighting not to fall to the ground. Had he used that first when she was closer, she knew she would have been out in an instant. It was even more potent than the one she had used on the guards.

But she was a mage and further away; her will countered it, barely.

Putting on as much speed as she could, she increased the distance between them.

Looking back, she saw he was following, but not running.

She dropped to a trot; one she could keep up for a long time.

At her next glance over her shoulder, she still saw him in the dim moonlight but, the distance widened. He wasn't running.

But did he have to?

He had reduced her to an under-shift and her spell book, on the edge of a desert.

**

Boom.

Panic surged through Ashes, jerking her out of her walking stupor.

Crackle Boom.

Relief flooded her. It was just thunder, not a surprise attack by the mage.

Still breathing hard, she glanced over her shoulder.

And relaxed even more. He wasn't there.

He had managed to stay with her for a full day, but she hadn't seen him in half a day.

Boom.

The wind and deluge hit.

In fear, she clutched her spell book. She'd treated each page so the ink wouldn't run, but having seen similar treated books in the library knew not to trust that.

Water started pooling, forming parallel lines on the ground.

This wasn't just a game trail. Carts used it from time to time.

Boom.

By the lords of hell, that rain was cold.

"**Kacharona.**"

**

Pain infested every joint of her body.

Cold gripped her.

She knew this pain; she'd botched a spell, again.

Opening her eyes, she saw water.

Oh yes, it had been raining. She had wanted to warm herself.

Ashes shivered. She was dying.

The ring sparkled on her finger.

She hadn't freed her soul, and she was dying. There was no reason now not to call on it. She spoke the name engraved on the ring. "Kocockto."

She gasped as the imp appeared nose to nose with her. The text didn't do it justice. It was far uglier than those pictures.

"I don't want to die," she managed to croak out.

"Good, I don't want you to die, either."

"I don't understand."

"Of course you don't. You don't have the mental capacity to understand things not spelled out for you. I'll spell it out. You have three curses on you, all of which give other demons claims on your soul higher than mine. Not only does your soul not go to me, it goes to one of my enemies, enhancing their position. No, I do not want you to die, either, you stupid pig. That is why my price for getting you out of this mess is going to be so cheap, you useless whore. All you need to do is promise to call me again once you are out of this mess and we talk about your next steps; slut that thinks she is a mage. Is it a deal?"

It was a cheap price. "Deal."

"Then crawl your sorry ass over to that bush. It is sweet-root. A couple of bites of it will energize you enough to stand. Once you have that in you, just follow that cart track you have been following, but too stupid to recognize until the rain pointed it out. Even someone as mentally weak as you should be able to accomplish that. There is a couple living in a shed who are grieving the loss of their children and will look kindly on you and feed you if you don't point out that is was their own foolishness that killed their kids. Be helpful and they will even give you something to wear. But make sure you learn you spells soon and leave no doubt in their minds they you are a mage, unless you want to end up as their slave, though in truth, you are little more than a worthless slave."

With no more than that, the imp vanished.

It, or rather he, it was grossly male, was right. There, just a few steps away, was sweet-root. How has she missed that?

Dare she?

She didn't really have a choice.

Every muscle screamed in agony as she pulled her way through the mud. That mess up should have killed her. Her power must have grown more than she had thought to absorb that much magic and live. Thankfully, the muddy sand around the bush moved easily, but there was no way to break it off in her condition.

She bit into it and tried not to gag at the bitter burning in her mouth. Sweet wasn't the taste, it was how that drug made you feel.

Then the euphoria hit.

She had just the presence of mind to let go of the root, pick up her spell book and start down the cart track.

When she fell again, it was at the doorstep of their shed. She closed her eyes.

Chapter VII

Getting Work

"Where do you think you're going?" said the middle-aged farmer from weeding his garden as Ashes stepped into the bright sunlight nearly a fortnight after arriving.

"It's time I get back on the road."

"Out of the question," he said, standing up, voice full of authority. "You haven't recovered enough. Don't worry. If your master comes looking, we never saw you."

Exasperation seeped into her voice. "For the last time, I am not a slave." This farmer and his wife were kind but insisted on thinking she was some run-away slave. She'd had enough. **"Kyayonday."**

Flame shot from her hands. Using that fire, she burned clear down to the dirt the center of the cart path, then let it die.

The man's eyes bugged, and he shrieked, "By the beard of Grammon! Sorcery!"

"I was not making up a story!"

She pointed the finger that had just spat fire. "I had just finished a bath when a stronger mage attacked my camp!"

He winced at the pointed finger.

"I am not some drug addicted tavern slut on the run!"

His eyes got wider as she emphasized her point with her hand pointing at him.

"I used sweet root only because I had to."

Terror written on his face; he fell to his knees. "I'm sorry, mistress, for not believing you."

Ashes sighed. "Get up. I am not a dark mage, and I am grateful to you for saving my life. If a mostly naked girl with Sweet Root stuck in her teeth showed up on my door, I might think the same thing. But I have to do some spells now, and you do not want those spells done near you."

From inside the shed came the woman's voice. "You can have that half loaf of bread for your travels. I'll bake more later. Give her some dried goat meat for her travels."

The woman was just as kind as her husband, but Ashes knew she wanted her gone. She didn't want a tavern slut living in her home, or a sorceress, for that matter. That had been part of her willingness to give her the dress when she asked.

The man jumped to his feet to do as his wife said.

He came out but had far more than his wife said to give her. A small sack of goat jerky and the half loaf of bread, belt, belt pouch with wooden spoon, and another empty small sack. Holding that sack out to her first, he nodded to her much battered spell book.

The generosity she knew was from him trying to make up for thinking she was only a slave. But she could not afford to turn them down. She slid her spell book into the sack, tied the belt around her waist, then tied both sacks to it, one on each hip.

He turned to his wife standing in the door. "Gea, give her your sandals. I'll have you a new pair made by bedtime."

Again Ashes didn't protest them putting themselves out that much for her, even though she knew keeping silent pushed her deeper into the black. Arriving barefoot with travel calloused feet would make getting work as a healer or mage more difficult.

The woman shrugged and slipped them off.

They were simple grass sandals and not well made. She doubted she would get even a week's walking out of them.

Never the less Ashes needed to balance the scales, especially if she was about to talk face to face to a demon. "I thank you. I have no money. But I am a good enough healer to fix your wife's gut trouble. Not permanently, but enough that she will get a few days, maybe a couple weeks, free of pain." Ashes didn't bother to explain that how long it lasted depended on how much coco root she ate. Like far too many things, a little of it once in a while improved your health, but using too much of it would kill you. It was undoubtedly a factor in why their kids kept dying young. As much as she wanted to explain that to them, the imp was right. Telling them that they were at fault would not convince them, but would make them angry.

"It has been hurting something fierce here lately. A few days relief would be welcome as long as it isn't drug that addle my mind."

"No, no drugs. Think of it as a rash on the inside, instead of the outside. I am using the same spell that clears up a rash on your skin but inside you instead. You have had that spell before?"

"No, never saw anything but a herb woman ever. Except for the tummy problem, I have always been healthy. I need to get rid of a rash; I use a poultice."

"That is best, and what I usually recommend unless the rash is very bad or in a place that using a poultice is not a good idea. You can't very well put a poultice on your insides, though. It is a simple healing spell, one of the first spells I learned during my apprenticeship. Shall I use it on you?"

She looked to her husband, who nodded. "Yes, please."

"Mesta Col."

"Oh! That felt strange, but is isn't hurting near so much."

"If you stick to eating only fresh fruits for a few days, even that might disappear for a while."

Her husband said, "We can do that. The first of the peaches are ripening."

"But the citadel pays the most for the first pick," she countered.

His voice became firm. "You getting back to top health is more important than getting a few more copper bits." He turned back to Ashes. "I am sorry I thought you just a runaway slave. Thank you for this."

"I fully understand. A runaway slave showing up on your door is far more likely that a Sorceress that lived through an ambush from a stronger mage. But I have to go. There is a spell I need to complete, and it is too dangerous for other people to be near me when I do it." She turned and headed down the cart track.

∗∗

"Kocockto."

"It's about time, slut. You have been well enough to call me for well over a day," the imp said, appearing. It was even uglier than she remembered.

"It cost you. Now you can't catch that courier and get the job directly but have to go through people that are going to take most of the commission."

"What in the names of the Lords of Hell are you talking about? And how does this help me get rid of those claims on my soul?"

"OK simpleton. In terms even you can understand. You need resources, badly, before doing anything, and you need to get them in a way that doesn't weigh against your soul. I cannot, and will not, help you in any way that goes against my own interest. Meeting both requirements leaves you very very few options. The best would have been to be at the citadel when the courier arrives. Now it is too late. You can't get there until after he leaves. There guard captain isn't going to offer it to you for even one coin in ten of what he is getting. He knows damn well he can find people that would do it for that. But even at that it is more coin than you have ever had at one time. And it will get you the right reputation in the right place to get more hire paying work."

The damned Imp laughed at her confusion.

"Listen up, stupid slave that thinks she is a sorceress. The ways of getting those curses off you are limited. First is, go to the right temple. They can free your soul, but at the cost of your life, the right is very painful, lasting for months. You are not going to do that, or we would not even be talking. Two of the curses are weak. If you pay the right mage, they will remove them for you. That takes far more than you currently have."

"And the third?"

"You killed a lot of people escaping from Black Water, some of it not necessary. Using the blood of more than one of your victims, mistress Gru put a rather nasty curse on you. There is no straightforward way of removing a justified blood curse. It can be removed, but the when and how changes with every action you take. You might as well not even consider it until after the other two curses are gone."

The imp leered at her and she fought not to vomit. "You need resources, you need power, and you need a means of increasing all of them before even considering trying to remove the easiest of them. There are plenty of such opportunities for a follower of the white, and a follower to the black would be looking for a strong enough master to remove them for her. But for you, my pet, opportunities are far fewer. If you miss this one, you are going to struggle just keeping yourself fed trying to reach the next unless you turn to whoring again."

The thought of whoring again sent a shiver down her spine. "What is this opportunity, and why should I trust anything you say?"

"This citadel that the peasants mention is roughly two days away. It houses mercenaries employed by the king to control this border. Sometime today a courier from the king will arrive with a purse and demands that the guard there eliminate a nest of goblins. That purse of coin is sufficient to do the job to this band. But the courier doesn't like them and would have paid someone else if there was anyone else there to do it. He will be gone before you can get there now. The mercenary captain's first choice it always to pay someone else to take the risk when it is cost effective to do so. You need to be there before he offers it to those he is considering contacting."

Ashes considered that, if the goblin nest was small, she could handle it.

"As for trusting me, only an idiot would do that. Don't trust me or anyone else. What you do know is that you are alive only because I wanted you to be. I have given you a plausible story on to why I want you to be, that if I can't have you, I can at least keep you out of my enemy's hands. Look for clues that back it up and ones the refute it. Make up your own mind how much is true."

He pointed down the cart trail. "If you come to the road before nightfall, back up and camp off the cart track. There is a nice, sheltered place for it. As long as you don't laze the morning away, you should make The Citadel by late evening. All this help is because I want to keep you out of my enemy's hands. But if you want more, I can do that, but it will cost you. Don't call on me unless you have finished this job and collected your pay, or you are willing to pay for my help. Pain and more, yours or someone else's."

The imp vanished.

How much had been true? One thing she knew, she would not call on him until after. The thought of that thing touching her sent a fear through her unlike anything ever had. It was almost enough to make her seek out a temple.

**

Late evening shadows pointed right at the keep the locals called the citadel, emphasizing its rundown, decrepit shape.

An icy shiver ran down Ashes' spine.

Not even a guard stood outside its weathered, battered wooden door or in front of the closed gate beside it.

She coughed.

Even the smell this far from the building spoke of the muck pile being left for far too long.

Yet it should have been what she expected. Mercenaries that would hire a mage instead of going after a group of goblins themselves are going to let other things go.

With each step forward, the smell got worse.

At the gate the door plate knocker was missing.

The rock she lifted from next to that door had marks where others had done the same.

Bam, bam, bam.

Her three knocks echoed inside, and she dropped the rock back where it had been.

The birds in the trees outside the keep went silent, and she could hear the sound of people in the distance.

She waited.

And waited.

And waited.

When the bird drowned out the sounds again, she picked up the rock and pounded the door again.

"Alright alright alright, Keep your sword sheathed, I'm coming."

That voice was slurred and right on the other side of the door.

She heard the bar grinding as it was slid back, then a bleary-eyed man smelling of cheap beer stood in the door. He smiled and leered, "Hi, Sweetness. You here for our party?"

She really missed her robes and head cover.

"No. My magic said you were hiring a mage to clear out some goblins. I am here to see if the pay is worth my time."

His slur got worse. "You don't be looking like no magister. Tell us another story."

Ashes sighed and raised her hand. She was getting a robe the moment this job was done.

"Kyayonday."

He fell back, landing on his ass as her whole right arm erupted into fire.

She pointed her flaming arm at him and thundered, "Go now. Tell your captain that the Sorceress Ashes of the Volcano would have words with him about doing a job."

"Yes, mistress, at once," the man stuttered out, scrambling to his feet, his slur gone.

A blanket and jug lay against the gate, showing that the guard had been napping and drunk enough to have ignored her first knock.

Only moments later, a dirty young man arrive that could be fifteen-years-old tops. "The captain will see you now. He sent me to take you to his office. He will be there shortly."

The boy's voice shook with fear.

But was it of the sorceress he was to escort, or of this captain? From the glances he gave her as the two of them walked through the outer courtyard and up a flight of stairs, it could have been either one.

Stale wine, mildewed paper and fish oil lamps assaulted her nose on opening the office door on the third floor.

"Have a seat, mistress. The captain will be here soon," he said his voice trembling more than before.

Both. He feared both.

Had this captain given him reason to fear them both, or was he just a fearful young man?

That question was still unanswered when the boy left the room.

Ashes turned a chair to face the door, then sat down. She glanced about the room at the four fish oil lamps.

"Canda Tomb."

All four wicks lit at once.

Ashes tried not to gag. That oil was old and not strained right.

As she considered putting them back out, the door opened and a bald scar-faced man missing an eye entered and looked her over.

"Ken was right. You don't look like much of a mage."

She shrugged. "What can I say? There are things even mages have to flee. One caught me at my bath. I just grabbed the first thing I could after getting out of there. I need to rebuild things before going back and reclaiming what is mine, so you get a deal."

Ashes paused, then took a deep breath. She put far more confidence into her voice and expression than she really felt. "Using magic, I found out you have a commission you would rather not do. You need a goblin nest cleared out. For a third of it, I'll go out there tomorrow and clear it for you."

"Your too late," the man said closing the door and leaning against it.

"You have done it?"

He shook his head. "No, my creditors were here before you. Between them and paying my men, more than three-fourths is already gone. I have put back one tenth as a bonus do be divided up among the men that go tomorrow. But you're right, I don't really want to risk them. It isn't their kind of fight. I am willing to hold off sending them for a day, if you are willing to do it for just the bonus I was holding back for them."

Ashes looked around the room. "A deal might be possible. That bonus, a room to work in for a week after I get back, enough of this parchment for a book, and access to all these maps to copy into that book, plus three meals a day for that week."

He looked around his office surprised, "These? Most are old and useless showing farms building and things that are not there anymore."

"Useless to you, not so useless to others." In truth, only a few of them would be of a benefit, but those would be very helpful to an outsider like herself.

"Ok, deal. But after you clear it out, you will escort one of my men there and prove that you cleared every goblin from the place." He extended his hand.

She took it and shook it once. "Show me what maps of the area and the cave you have, and give me every detail you know about this nest."

Thick black blood squirted her eyes as Ashes sliced her knife across the goblin shaman's throat, and his grip around her throat relaxed.

She could breathe again.

His relaxing his grip allowed her to shift her own grip. She drove the small dagger up through his jaw and into his brain.

The last goblin in the cave died.

It was over.

Demons! that blood tasted rank.

She dropped to the ground and looked at the bloody mess of her skirt and left leg. She would live. Using every bit of magic she had left; she could even heal it enough to make it back to the Citadel.

Good enough.

She looked at the taller than average goblin body, her blade still stuck in his skull, another blade covered in her blood in his hand. He had been a crafty old bastard and far more capable than goblin shamans were supposed to be. Not one of her spells could touch him and she had been hard pressed to resist his.

"Mesta Col."

It wasn't enough, but she stopped bleeding. She used her remaining cantrip, then stood up.

It hurt like she was in the hands of the lords of the abyss, but she could move.

Taking his blade from his hand, the power tingled her fingers.

That was it. It had been that blade. Somehow it had let him turn her spells. She had to figure out if she could make this power hers. If she could, this alone would make the entire job worth it.

With a wince, she squatted down to see if his body had other treasures.

Nothing: only a near empty coin purse and the sheath for the dagger that was of use to her.

"Damn you to the depth of hell!" she screamed at the shaman, then felt like a fool.

She didn't know where these had hidden whatever loot they had.

She began making her way out of the cave and past the three chambers of goblin bodies whose throats she had slit after putting the whole nest to sleep.

The chieftain, and most powerful warrior, lay in the outermost chamber. He was their clan's first line of defense.

His body had no treasure either.

It did have a spear that she could use as a crutch to get her back to the Citadel.

She let out a sigh. She could not stay and search in her present condition. That would have to be put off until she came back with the guard to prove the job was done. Undoubtedly, they would demand a large share of it.

"Festo's left nut!" she exclaimed, stepping from the cave and seeing the long shadows stretched before her. Surely it hadn't taken her as long as that to do the job.

She looked back into the mouth of the cave with a shiver. The idea of sleeping around that many dead goblins made her want to vomit. She turned her head back to the trail that led to the road. In her condition, and with no spells, dare she sleep on the road? There were many things in these woods far more dangerous than goblins.

She had to make the Citadel if she left here.

Then another doubt hit. Would they open the gate after dark? She shook that thought off. Even if they didn't, camping outside those gates would be safer than on the road.

That decided things.

**

Leg burning in agony, she sighted torches in the distant.

The gate?

Lift the spear butt, put it one more step forward, and she took another step.

Leaving that goblin cave had been dumb.

Step by agonizing step, she closed in on the light.

It was the gate.

Moreover, she could hear the sound of a party inside. Movement in the shadows to the right of the gate caught her eye.

"By Festo's left nut, they have a guard posted," she murmured to herself.

"Whose out there!" demanded the guard.

She raised her voice, "Sorceress Ashes. I've finished the job you hired me for."

"Well, come into the light so I can see you."

"I am trying, but I'm injured. I am moving very slowly."

"Injured?"

"Their shaman had a talisman that stopped my magic. He and I got into a knife fight." She took one more step. "He got in a good cut before I finished him." And another step.

"But they are all dead now?" his voice called, full of questions.

"Yes." One more pain-filled step forward. "He was the last and the toughest." She stepped one more step closer.

"Ok, I can see you now." He started walking forward. "Looks like he did a number on the leg."

"Given some time to recover, I can heal it."

He reached for her spear. "Give me that. Then wrap an arm around me. I'll get you to the captain. He and everyone else are in the banquet hall. We got fresh beer in today,"

Ashes released the spear, and the guardsman slipped his arm around her, taking most of her weight.

A kick to the gate from the massive, bearded man, and it swung open. He all but carried her through the small opening.

"It won't be long now, just to the left there."

Light shone into the court through an opened door and Ashes lean more into the strong arms of the guard as they made their way toward it.

The captain sat at the head of the table full of drunken men toying with a scarf.

"Is it done?" he asked as they came to a stop in front of him.

"Yes," she breathed out.

The man holding her slammed her forward onto the table hard, and that scarf in the captain's hand was stuffed in her mouth, her arms wrenched behind her. Terror filled her as she tried to fight as two men with strip of cloths bound her fist close then put on mage glove to keep her from opening them.

Her screams as they tore her clothes from her body never got past the scarf stuffed in her mouth.

Chapter VIII

Betrayed

Agony burned through Ashes as she opened one eye and saw blue sky and clouds.

How was it that she was still alive?

These brutes planned for her to die from the moment she returned to the Citadel. They gloated over first using her to get rid of the goblins, then using her up afterwards.

Don't kill her yet. I haven't had my turn, had been said more than once.

She tried moving her hand, and nearly passed out in agony.

The memory came.

A man holding out her arms as a massive blacksmith hammer smashed her hands before they took off the mage glove that kept her fist closed.

Her hands were useless. She could not remove the gag in her mouth.

That stench.

This was the muck pit. They thought her dead.

Had she screamed when she tried to move?

She didn't remember.

Maybe the gag had worked, and no one heard it.

Violent shakes started. If someone discovered her alive, the raping would continue until she was dead.

But she was dying now. She could feel that.

And a demon waited to claim her, that would make what she just went through seem just a warmup.

With an effort that told her, her time was short, and the agony making her vision swim, she turned her head to the side and managed to get her hand up where she could see it.

That hand was a ruined mess. She concentrated, focusing on the ring and not the mangled mess that was her hand.

Kocockto.

The ugly demon appeared nose to nose with her.

"How can anyone as dumb as you have lived as long as you have? It takes a rather stupid slut to walk up to a band of mercenaries helpless and not expect to be raped and then killed. I could not believe you were doing anything that stupid. I thought all the time I was investing in you gone when you did something that dumb."

She didn't answer. The grotesque creature was right. It had been as dumb a move as taking off her clothes for Hammer had been.

"But all isn't completely lost. I can save you. And there is something you can offer me beside your own soul for me to do that."

Her heart raced. She wasn't about to jump for one demon, only to give another an even stronger hold on her, and this imp knew it. But there was a hook in it. There had to be.

"Here's the deal I am offering you for that help, you miserable, stupid slut. Every man here wrong you enough to allow you a vengeance curse, offering those souls to a demon. You will cast that spell summoning a demon from my faction strong enough to rip those souls out of their bodies. As all of those that wronged you are already condemned, so calling a demon for vengeance doesn't bind your soul to me of even darken it that much. But for my help in setting this up, you include in that bargain with that the demon you summon, that it must give me two of the souls it claims."

She could do this. The men deserved that. Her vengeance was justified, so she could use a demon to exact it. It would buy her the time she needed to free her soul of both this imp and the curses she had on her.

"You are truly one dumb slut. There is more to it than you are taking into account. I am going to tell you just how stupid you are. You are going to agree to this deal, and you will be my plaything for the next two weeks."

Her blood froze. Nothing she had been through could be as bad as handing herself over to an imp to be his toy. What are the side effect of being raped by a demon? How is it that human live through that?

What she read in her demon research came back to her. For a human to survive being rape the demon empowered them with healing energy. To save her life, she had to agree to being raped, not just now, but for the next two weeks. Could her mind survive that?

The imp laughed at her. "I will even tell you another of the hooks you're overlooking. If you fail to keep this bargain after making it, I get top claim on your soul. You see, this bargain is a win-win for me. One way or another, I get another soul and grow more powerful. I would rather have two than one, so I do want you to succeed."

The foul creature gloated. "Your time is running out. I act within a few breaths, or you die. Become my toy for the next two weeks or start being the permanent possession of a bigger badder demon. Shall I start healing you?"

She hated this imp, but knew she had no choice. She nodded.

The bargain was struck.

The Imp said something, and suddenly there was silence.

Her terror rose. With a silence spell in the pit, the Imp didn't have to worry about someone hearing what was happening down here.

With Ashes screaming into the silence, the evil creature pulled both her mangled hands up in front of her face and began licking them as a child might lick a sweet.

Pain beyond even having them smashed with the hammer shot through her, but the spell prevented any sound from being made.

Except the sounds made by the imp.

"It's too bad I can't listen to your screams," the gravelly voice whispered to her. "I have waited so long for them trapped in that ring."

With more strength that she suspected the creature no taller than her forearm to have, he twisted those arms, flipping her onto her face. Muck flooded her mouth and nose, and she struggled to raise her face from it.

The moment she got a breath, the damn imp wrenched her arms behind her, forcing her arm up and her face back down into the muck.

She fought for breath but only got more muck, as the imp kept her arms high behind her.

Just as she was on the edge of passing out, Kocockto rolled her back onto her back, ripped off her gag and punched her in the gut.

Muck spewed from her lungs, and she began to vomit.

She could not bring her arms forward; the dam creature had tied her hands behind her while she was face down in the muck.

No sooner than she cleared her lung, the massive cock hanging down for the grotesque beast was shoved in her mouth and throat, cutting off her air with his hands on both sides of her face.

That violation of having a that vile thing in her was far beyond any rape she had ever experienced.

His cum flooded her lung and stomach, but his cock stayed in place so she could not vomit it up. She had never imagined something that tasted so rank.

"You are not dying even if you can't breathe. Blood, cum or even excrement, the body fluids of a demon can heal its victim and keep them alive."

He pulled his cock out of her mouth, and she gasped for air.

Slapping her face, he said, "You are now strong enough to stand and make it to a room no one now uses. You will now come with me to a place I can continue this uninterrupted."

He was right. He had healed her that much while raping her.

With that, the ugly creature fastened a slave collar and leash around her neck, and smiled at her. "Of course you can disobey. In which case you will have broken our agreement, and I am free to kill you and take your soul, as I will then have top claim on it for that broken agreement."

She shuddered. This imp had her exactly where it wanted her. With an effort, she managed to get to her feet. She might not be in danger of dying any more, but was far from steady.

"Good slut. You're right. Nothing I can do to you right now if you obey is anywhere near being in the same class of what I get to do to you if I get your soul. But nevertheless, the next few days are going to be far, far worse than anything you have ever imagined."

Of that Ashes had no doubt.

"It is morning now and people are beginning to move. Not the guard, they're all hung over from the party last night. Follow me, but one thing more."

With a wave of his hand, the muck took the shape of a body, then the body took on her features. Then it changed to look to be rat-eaten. "Wouldn't want someone to notice you gone now, would we? I'll make it look more rat-eaten every day until there is nothing left."

Pulling her by the leash, he led her up the steps out of the muck pit, then up some stairs.

She tried thinking of some way out or to even delay it, but nothing came to mind as he led her through an opened door and up stairs after stairs. The door he opened, opened on a room full of old furniture, much of it rotted.

The Imp untied her hands. "That bench up there. Pull it down and put it in the middle of the room."

Ashes began to cry. He wanted a whore's couch with straps on it. Such was often called a raping couch. She had no real choice but to get it.

With work, she got it to the center of the room, her sob muffled by the imp's spell.

**

"Have you learned your lesson, you stupid slut?" Kocockto asked.

Ashes' eyes focused on that face that had kept her bound in that same position for two weeks now. The foul creature went on, "It would be in your best interest to agree to be my slave for all eternity, rather than risking messing up summoning an evil that is greater than I. You are not very bright. The chance of you not bargaining away your soul to something that has a far greater capacity for inflicting pain than I, is very small."

Its claw cut the strap of the gag as easily as it had cut her flesh so many times, and the silence spell vanished. She could hear the birds outside and people in the courtyard. He pulled the nasty bit from her mouth.

Instead of shoving his member in her mouth as she was expecting, Kocockto spoke, and Ashes realized that the imp's voice was only in her head and had always only been there. How had she missed that? "Decide now, slave. Take a risk that something far more cruel than I will get you, on the slight chance you might win free, or admit I own you. Either way, I win, either you or someone else."

"Release me. I will do the summoning I agreed to, once I get my spell book and memorized the spell."

"So be it. But you don't need your book, just the spell. I have it here. They never noticed the page being taken."

His claw cut through the strap holding her right arm up behind her, then the left. Fresh agony shot through her.

"Such a shame. There are a lot of things I would have loved doing to you in that position. I had barely gotten started." The agony of having her ankle cut loose forced a groan from her.

"Careful. Things are in a balance. You don't want someone to find you alive before you get that spell done. If you die and it is your fault before that summoning, I will get your soul, so long as I am not the one to cause it. I am making sure you understand, so there is no doubt that if you mess up before you complete that spell and die, your soul is mine from that point on." Kocockto pointed, and she saw a bowl of fruit, the page from her spell book, the chalk, candle and other things she needed to do the spell.

When she looked back, the imp was gone, and her ring pulsed. Was that the secret? Did she have to have the imp summoned to pull the ring from her finger? It had to be more complicated, but it was a place to start.

Her hair still held her to the post and on examining the strap there was no easy way of getting loose. The strap had been riveted there not just tied. Not only that, but straps still wrapped her hands, keeping her fingers immobile.

Her heart pounded.

Damn that imp. If someone came in now, she would be helpless. They would tie her to that bench and have another party, but this time, make sure of her. She began chewing at the knots in the straps wrapping her hand as the agony in her long unused limb continued.

More voices outside sent a shiver of terror through her. The voices came closer then moved away.

She worked those knots loose with her teeth. In time, her right hand came free. With that one free, the left came loose much faster.

Next came the strap with her matted hair braided to it. Damn, her knife was on her spell book out of reach. She dare not drag the bench with the silence spell gone.

Agony burned in her as she stood and left leg gave out and hit the floor with a thud.

She froze and waited, but it was difficult to hear anything with her heart thundering in her ears.

When no one came to investigate, she made it to the fruit bowl and her spell.

**

As the sun dropped toward the horizon the following day, Ashes looked at her two diagrams on the wooden floor drawn in chalk and blood; one rat's blood to confine the demon, and one in her own to shield her once she released the demon from that confinement.

She shivered.

This was as dangerous as any magic she had ever done. It wouldn't protect her from any of the greater demons, so she had to be careful not to open it up to one. Nor, dare she call on one by a name she had read. Either the names were of far greater power than these protections could hold, or they were booby-trapped, and the master of the demon you called, and not that demon arrived.

Her heart pounded, her pulse loud in her ears.

It had to be a general calling to a type of demon, not a specific one. But that had dangers too.

She still hadn't settled on the type when she memorized this spell last night. If it wasn't strong enough to do the job, she was dead as soon as they defeated it. But if she got an answer of one too strong, it would break her barrier and take her as its first victim.

A woman singing in the courtyard, waking her that morning, gave her the answer she needed, a succubus. Ashes rubbed her finger alone the edge of the pattern to contain her. Most of the magic available to a succubus worked only on men, so this confinement should be especially effective now that she modified it to specifically hold such, and not just any demon. The less power that the demon could wield against her the better.

Ashes didn't need a mirror to know that a cruel smile had crossed her face. The rapist being killed by their lust. Few punishments could be more fitting.

Even better, it would be easier to confine it to just the men and to leave the women and children here alone. Ashes did not need those deaths added to her own tally.

She looked at the window again.

Almost time.

This spell could only be used after dark, and the task must be one that can be done in a night.

She picked up the dagger she had used to draw her blood and struck it with the flint. It rang out louder than she liked, but the spark from it was a good one and landed in the lent she had gathered. It only took a cantrip from there to ensure she had a small blaze in that lint. She lit the small rushlight and set it aside and put the lint flame out.

The room got slowly darker.

When the only light she had to see by was the rushlight, she stood to hang an old canvas over the window.

But first a look out now that it was too dark for someone to see her at the window.

This was not the side that had the gate or the hall entrance. Nor had anyone bothered to light the torches out there. She shivered and quickly hung the canvas before it got dark enough out so that even that tiny rushlight could be detected. Someone coming to investigate a light that should not be there was the last thing she needed.

Ashes sat and used her mind calming exercise as she watched the rushlight slowly burn down. When it reached just a nub, she lit a candle with it. Lifting that candle she stood and lit the eight other candles she had placed were the spell required.

The room was much brighter than she liked.

She had no choice.

Taking her seat in the center of her protections, she began chanting her spell, hoping to get it finished before someone discovered her.

Chapter IX

Kayomaya Taskimona

Ashes finished her chant.

A beautiful yet hideous bat winged creature appeared, hissing inside the confinement circle. It raised lust even in her, with a face and torso of a heartbreakingly beautiful raven-haired woman of olive complexion.

"Why call me, woman?" the creature hissed at her.

"Kocockto," Ashes called.

The imp appeared inside Ashes' protective pattern. That worried her. It should not have happened. Kocockto should have appeared outside her pattern, but not in the one confining the succubus.

The succubus's eyes narrowed at the sight of the imp, and she hissed, her clawed feet tearing gouges in the floor. "Kocockto, is this your doing? Is this slut your?" she pointed at Ashes.

"Yes, I am responsible, Most Evil of Mistresses, Tormentor of Slaves. My associate here has over a dozen souls she can claim vengeance on and offer them to you. And as go between I am to get two!"

The demon, nearly half again as tall as Ashes, stood taller and hissed, "You want me to hunt them down and you dare try and claim two?"

"That is the deal I struck with her."

"I won't do it."

That was the last thing Ashes expected. What demon turns down souls offered to it?

"Oh why, Most Evil Mistress? Hunting these men would be nothing for one of your power, and the pay great."

An ugly, terrifying laugh burst from her. "Because they are coming here. They will kill your slut and destroy this power holding me, and I will have them all and you get nothing. I will even get the soul of your slut instead of you. I just have to wait."

"No!" Ashes screamed out. "I can and will send you back. This is my power keeping you here."

"You think you can send me back if I don't want to go before they come in and kill you? No, that isn't going to happen."

It had to be a bluff. "Then we will see," Ashes said with confidence. "You risk losing all those souls if I succeed. Are you going to chance it?"

"Yes, unless you offer me something worth those three souls, I would claim just by waiting."

There it was. This bitch wanted something, and this was her bargaining ploy. Now understanding what was going on, Ashes stood straighter. "What is it you want?"

"To bond with one of the souls instead of killing them so I can stay here past dawn. The summoning spell you chose prevents me from doing that without your permission."

"And have you kill me the instant you are bonded? I don't think so. Nor am I about to let a demon as powerful as you roam the land completely free."

Voices in the courtyard let both know that their time was getting short. Yet it also presented an opportunity Ashes hadn't considered. What deal could she make with these men not to release the succubus?

The succubus hissed. "Very well, not free, and I swear not to kill you. I will be no more than one hundred paces from the person I bond to. But you must give me five days before you try and kill them, and if you come within that one-hundred-paces, I will hurt you even if I can't kill you."

Every evil this creature did before Ashes hunted down and killed who she bonded to would be counted against her, darkening her soul even more. Yet she had spells that reached beyond that one hundred paces range.

The voices got closer.

"To seal this deal, I would need your true name."

"The imp said it. Most Evil Mistress, or Kayomaya in our language, Taskimona, which is Tormentor of Slaves in yours."

Men were climbing the steps.

"Kayomaya Taskimona, I accept the deal you have offered if you agree to harm only those in this citadel you are entitled to. Bond to whom you wish and kill these men, claiming their souls for yourself."

"I accept."

The candles confining the dark beast of a woman went out and the door bust open.

The demon moved

Blood curdling scream filled the room as she reached the men. They cut off and she was out the door.

Kocockto laughed and vanished.

Kocockto's maniacal laughter and disappearance froze Ashes' blood.

She was so screwed.

Screaming on the stairs started and ended.

Breathing hard, Ashes turned that way, holding her dagger before her.

Per their agreement, she could not kill whoever this demon, Kayomaya Taskimona, bonded to for five days.

But that didn't mean that the man she bonded to could not kill her!

That had been a stupid oversite.

Her panting got faster.

Kayomaya would certainly make sure he did so. And Ashes was naked, and without her spells, or spell book, trapped in her protection with only the dagger she used to cast the spell. She was easy meat for any warrior.

She stared at her ring glinting brightly on the hand holding her dagger in horror. The things that Imp had done to her were but a pale shadow of what was in store for her now.

A diamond appeared on the gold ring as she watched.

That, she had not expected.

Goose bumps ran up her arm as she felt the power of the imp grow. Nor that.

Then another diamond appeared in the ring.

Two already? Did that mean he would not get her, and her soul would not be part of Kayomaya's payment to him when the man killed her? Or was her soul an extra treat for him?

No, she corrected that thought, he would not get an extra soul.

Screaming further away was cut short.

But there was no chance that Kayomaya wasn't planning to have her killed. Every moment the demon was here beyond completing the rightful vengeance Ashes summoned her for, pushed Ashes further and further onto the Black Path.

One more scream cut short highlighted that thought.

She had to banish that demon or give up the Gray Path, and this Kayomaya had no plans of being banished.

Damn it. Why hadn't she included not having someone kill her in her bargaining!

With the weight of this summoning against her now, there was little doubt as to which demon would claim her soul if she died now. Having the strongest claim on Ashes' soul was one more reason that this Kayomaya had to see her dead now if she could.

So why had this demon given a man's soul to the imp, when she was planning to collect a woman's and could have kept the man's for herself? From everything she knew of this breed, they could extract more power and pain from a man's soul rather than a woman's.

Or was there a way out?

Running for it was out of the question. Kayomaya could not kill her, but if Ashes step one step beyond her protective circle before the demon was bound, that creature could be here in moments and break her legs, leaving her easy picking for whoever she bound herself to.

Maybe that was the out. With the men that were climbing the stairs now dead, most of the men were beyond that one-hundred-pace limit.

Another fainter scream proved she was beyond that limit.

"Kocockto."

"You called, slut?"

The demon had changed. He was still as small as he had been, but was more substantial, with a greater presence, and sense of evil menace. Had he been suppressing it or had the new souls made him more vile?

"I need you to tell me the moment she bonds to someone."

"There is no need for that," came a female voice from behind her.

Ashes whirled, and lust almost pulled her from the circle. The demon was even more beautiful than before. Ashes had to force herself to remain in place.

"There is only one person left alive I can bond to. Ashes, daughter of the miller of Oak Well and the slave he bought for a wife, I bind myself to you."

Kayomaya stepped across the protective circle as if it wasn't there.

The thought flashed through Ashes that she had unknowingly consented to this demon crossing that boundary when she gave her permission to bond to who she wanted.

"But I am a woman," Ashes scream. "Your magic doesn't work on me!" The clawed hand squeezed down on her arm, ripping muscle, forcing that scream into a high pitch shriek of pain as the demon lifted her from the floor.

"Who ever gave you that idea was dead wrong," the beast said, holding her up eye to eye. "Some of it works much better on men, it is true, but all work on women too. And you are all equally disgusting. Yet still I would have chosen one of those men and given you to the imp, but for one thing. You have magic. Magical toys are much more fun to play with, if I can keep from killing you."

Kayomaya tossed Ashes into the air with no effort, and she hit the ceiling. Then, as she fell back, grabbed her by her thigh with the demon's claw ripping into her flesh and tearing even more muscle on her way down.

Ashes screamed again. She almost didn't notice breaking her right wrist hitting the floor as she hung there, head a hand's breadth off the floor.

Kayomaya let Ashes go, and her face slammed into the floor.

As she lay there, face down, panting, the clawed toe of the monster entered her ass.

Ashes screamed as it cut deep inside her.

The scream became a shriek as the monster put her full weight on that foot, tearing that claw through her and into the wooden floor. Blood gushed from her groin when the claw pulled back, tearing her flesh, then the creature withdrew.

Ashes stared in horror at the blood gushing out of her groin. The monster had cut an artery when she ripped Ashes open.

"Get over here, Toy, and start licking some of this healing juice so we can continue our fun and games."

The succubus sat on a trunk, legs spread, stroking her cunt with her claw.

Despair overwhelmed Ashes. She helped this monster torture her here, or she died, and the creature could inflict far worse torture on her when she had her soul.

She stretched her good arm toward the succubus. Then screamed in agony as she pulled herself a cubit closer to the creature.

"If you can't do better than that, it is best you die soon and I take you to where I can have some real fun with you."

The agony was unbelievably worse as she forced her mangled arm and broken wrist along with her torn up leg to assist in moving her across the floor.

"Better. You might make it here before you bleed out now."

A jolt went through her as she touched her own circle of power, giving her a fresh new agony causing her to curl into a ball.

Evil laughter filled the room. "No, my little Toy, no curling up, or you die."

Ashes could hardly believe her circle had survived this demon crossing it several times. It took her nine breaths to focus and remove it with her life gushing out with her pulse from between her legs.

Then the power blocking her was gone.

She lurched forward with a scream.

"Good, my little Toy. Keep it up and you might make it this far alive."

Ashes screamed and lurched forward another cubit.

Another scream, another cubit, again and again.

The succubus's knees were now closed, and its clawed hands rested on them.

"Tell me how important it is to you to lick my cunt."

Damn. the bitch wanted her to beg. Knowing full well that it gave this creature even more power over her, Ashes said, "Please, Mistress, let me lick your cunt."

"No, you will do more than just lick it, or you will do nothing."

"Please Mistress, I promise to do all I can to give you pleasure," Ashe cried in desperation.

"A demon's barging then, this time and every time I desire, you will do your best to please me if I let you taste me now."

Ashes knew she had no choice but to swear. "Yes, Mistress."

Her knees parted, and she leaned back, "Then taste, and seal your fate at my Toy, slave and servant of evil."

Utterly defeated, Ashes moved between those knees.

She would forever walk the dark path now, if she survived, there could be no doubt of that.

Follow Ashes' quest for vengeance against all who wronged her in;
Ashes of Evil
coming soon

Milton Keynes UK
Ingram Content Group UK Ltd.
UKHW042002281024
450365UK00003B/98